PARTNERSHIP OF CRIME

A Novel

Fred Witt

Fred Witt is the author of three nonfiction books.
This is his debut novel.
He is a lawyer and lives in Phoenix, Arizona

ISBN: 1493759817
ISBN-13: 9781493759811
Library of Congress Control Number: 2013921597
CreateSpace Independent Publishing Platform
North Charleston, South Carolina

www.fredwitt.com

PARTNERSHIP OF CRIME

A Novel

FRED WITT

For my children

CHAPTER ONE

My dream of becoming a lawyer, fueled by my desire to help others, is being shattered before it can even take form. Failure is a demanding master and I feel like the ruined clay on the potter's wheel. With adversity a constant headwind, I have learned by necessity that, in order to survive, I must turn it to my advantage. Unbowed, and against long odds, I will not quit and submit. I started life near the bottom, but I am driven not to stay there. I will never let adversity have the last word.

My epic legal journey is immediately, and abruptly, derailed. "There are no changes. You are still on the waiting list, Mr. Pearson," advises the raspy voice at the law school admissions office. Pausing, in a way that causes me maximum pain, she asks, "Is there anything else I can do for you?" It is late April and I call regularly only to receive this same message. I desperately want to be a lawyer, but reality is in my way. With low B grades in college and an average score on the law school aptitude test, I will be lucky to even be considered, much less accepted. Despite this clarity, my emotions have been in a state of turmoil for months, with no relief in sight. What more can be taken away from me when I have nothing?

The waiting is unbearable, made worse when friends ask me "have you heard yet?" The failure tape runs overtime in my mind. With adversity a constant companion, how can my hope for a better life be doused like putting water to flame while I am taking the steps necessary to turn that hope into reality? Is the life I experienced so far really the way it will always be? Why is life so dark and cruel? Despite my best efforts to overcome, will nothing ever change?

The other applicants I know received their law school acceptance letters in March. Their pursuit is complete and their walk and demeanor reflect joy and relief. It seems like those accepted have a common theme. They have been preparing a lifetime for entry into law school, supported and encouraged by parents who are professors, engineers, bankers or members of some other professional class. They can write and speak in a manner reflective of constant learning. Imagining they were buildings, I can tell they have a solid foundation with bricks laid neatly one on top the other. They are comfortable in their skin and confident of their abilities. No doubt able to face off against the challenges that lie ahead.

More than a few are of the most elevated stature and in the ruling legal class. They are second or third generation lawyers-in-waiting, with legal moms and dads inspiring them daily. Even their family outings were filled with tales of legal discourse and courtroom battles won. When I visited, I would stop and admire their houses. They were neat in appearance, colored with flowers in bloom and freshly painted. Whenever I walked inside, there were shelves with books of all shapes and sizes. I would touch them like they were some strange, exotic object, and wonder about the knowledge and wisdom within the leather-bound covers and beyond my reach. They had so much food in the kitchen. Fresh apples and bright yellow bananas were on display for anyone to eat whenever they desired. There were cereal boxes with brands advertised on television.

But that is not my world and none of it applies to me. My parents, older and the product of the depression, are uneducated and unprepared for the challenges of life. When they were growing up, a college education was not only unrealistic it was unthinkable. Their only goal was to survive the harshness of rural farm life. My father was an angry workaholic with whom alcohol did not agree. My mother must have been mentally ill because I have not had a conversation with her since age nine. As a child, I lived in silence and hunger. My father I didn't want to talk to and my mother I could not talk to. My home was one you ran from, not to. I had to leave in order to survive. I desperately wanted a normal life, but circumstances wouldn't allow. I was set up for a lifetime of failure. By what means does a child escape?

Swirling in this world of low expectations, my dreams of becoming a lawyer began in high school on a path parallel to normal reality. The legal journey that starts in law school appeared in the distance not out of ambition, but out of necessity. You see, I was a client first, well before I could even dare to entertain the audacious idea of going to law school and becoming a lawyer. I had to defend myself before I could defend anyone else.

"Registration and license," the officer barked.

"But officer, I wasn't doing anything wrong."

"Gee, kid, I've never heard that one before. Now give me your registration and license and turn your engine off," the officer demanded.

It takes me an eternity to produce the requested documentation, since my vehicle registration is stuffed in a small plastic bag in the back of my license plate frame. The officer waits impatiently while I fumble, finally producing a soiled and crumpled pink state-issued form.

I can't afford a car, so I ride an older, used motorcycle to get to work at a downtown retail store. My familiar pattern is to travel North down a one-way street in the left-hand lane and park on the left-hand side of the road, just before the intersection. Three lanes wide and with cars angle parked, there is a small space available for my two-wheeled vehicle. One motorcycle will fit, and I have little competition. With no parking meter to feed, I have unlimited parking on a busy street in the downtown business district of the Midwest town where I live. My minimum-wage budget will not allow otherwise.

On the day in question, I get off work at five-thirty p.m. and walk to my sun-faded gold motorcycle tucked in the corner. With the silver tape visible on the seat, I have little concern it will be stolen. After two failed tries on the kick-starter, there is a moment where failure is real and despair likely. On the third thrust downward, the bike reluctantly fires and starts with a cloud of blue smoke. Needing to turn right to head East towards home, I aim the bike parallel to the crosswalk, rev the engine and slowly drive across two lanes of traffic. After spending an ever-so-slight moment in the right-hand lane, I negotiate an immediate right turn from Twelfth Street onto Main. Right in front of a police officer staring in disbelief at my antics and waiting to pounce. My life of challenge is about to get another dose of adversity. Oh crap.

"I'm giving you a ticket charging you with making an improper right turn. Please read the ticket I've just written you."

I look down and mutter something unintelligible.

"What did you say, son? I want you to sign and acknowledge you did this and are guilty."

"I won't do that, officer."

"Why not? I caught you red-handed in the act. I saw it with my own eyes. You are guilty and I want you to sign the ticket and admit your guilt."

"No."

"What do you mean, no?"

"I didn't do anything wrong and I won't admit it."

"Son, I'm giving you this ticket. If you won't sign and admit guilt, you'll be going to traffic court and facing a judge. Why don't you save yourself the trouble?"

"Thanks, but no thanks. I won't do it."

"Okay, then. I'm completing the court portion of this ticket and ordering you to appear before a judge at municipal court on Thursday, September 15th at ten a.m."

"All rise. The court is now in session. Municipal Judge Carter presiding."

"The first case on the docket is City v. Pearson. Mr. Pearson, you have been charged with making an illegal right turn and thereby endangering pedestrians, a Class Two offense under the Municipal City Code. How do you plead?"

"Not Guilty, Your Honor."

"How old are you, son?"

"Just turned seventeen, Your Honor."

"You don't look that old and I have to ask. That makes you an adult in traffic court and you can go trial. Do you have a lawyer or are your parents here?"

"No sir. I'm here alone. If I got into this mess, I have to get myself out."

"So, why don't you just admit what you did and pay your fine?"

"Because I don't feel I did anything wrong."

"Well then, I will set a trial date for Tuesday, November 1, at one p.m. But let me warn you, Mr. Pearson, there are additional court costs and a fine imposed if you lose. Bring your money, the bailiff collects immediately."

After the hearing concludes and the black-robed figure walks gracefully out and disappears through a side door, I slump, alone, on the cold wooden courtroom bench. Panic ensues. My heart is racing and my breathing is labored. I have nowhere to turn, no one to seek out and ask for advice. I can't shake the thought of the virtually certain outcome — a stern judge waiting to "teach the kid a lesson" and impose a fine I can't pay. The words "you can't fight city hall" and "give up, it's a losing battle" repeat over and over in my mind. Why am I so stubborn? Why won't I give up and give in? Why don't I just do what the officer and the judge has each suggested and let it go and get it over with? They are experienced adults who see the situation for what it is. I am a kid with nothing who has no chance. I am screwed.

I return to the scene of the alleged crime and sit on the corner of Twelfth Street and Main and stare. I don't feel I did anything wrong, but how can I, will I, prove it? I turned right in the turning lane just in front of me. Thinking longer, it occurs to me I am charged with a violation of the Municipal City Code. If I violated it that means there must be one. Maybe if I can find the Code, there might be something in it helpful to my case.

I mount my motorcycle and drive *straight* this time. I take the long way around the large city blocks. I make the five-minute drive over to City Hall where there is plenty of parking for those with city business or those in city trouble. I walk up to the teller window and politely ask if there is such a thing as a City Code. The librarian-looking lady with her reading glasses chained securely around her neck says yes there is, but offers nothing more. I then ask if I can get a copy. She brusquely replies they are only available for sale for five dollars. I pull a crumpled ten-dollar bill out of my jeans pocket, hand it to her and ask if she can make change. As if believing kids shouldn't have such things, she reluctantly hands me a little blue book with the official words Municipal City Code printed in large black letters and five bucks change. I get the distinct impression she doesn't sell many blue books to seventeen-year-old kids. This is a domain for grown-ups with official city business.

I thumb through the thick book and find the traffic code section. I read through dense, meaningless detail and I find an offense labeled "improper turns." An improper turn is defined as a turn from an improper lane. There is also another offense described as an "improper change of lanes," which is the failure to allow thirty feet to pass before making a change from one lane to the next lane over.

I start my trial preparation by purchasing a large white poster board and colored markers. I draw the intersection of Twelfth Street and Main on the poster board. Demonstrative evidence drawn on a poster board seems the thing to do, but I have no idea if it really matters. Doing something feels better than doing nothing.

As my November trial date nears, my friends are excited about Homecoming while all I can think about is my trial coming.

❖

I am told by one intrepid soul that my only hope of prevailing is if the police officer fails to show up. My heart sinks as I meet my Officer Hernandez sitting in the back of the courtroom. It is just the two of us. He says it is his day off and he is not too happy to be in court, but he is duty-bound to show up. Just my luck, a diligent officer eager to appear in court and testify against me. If my Plan A is to get a dismissal by default, what is my Plan B? His serious law enforcement expression says it all. I am going down in flames.

Abraham Lincoln knew what he was talking about when he said, "A man who represents himself has a fool for a client." From my limited experience, I will add "and an idiot for a lawyer."

"All rise. The court is now in session. Municipal Judge Carter presiding."

"I will start today with the trial scheduled in the case of City v. Pearson. Are both Mr. Pearson and the charging police officer present in the courtroom?"

"Yes and yes."

"Well then, Mr. Pearson do you have a lawyer with you?"

"No, Your Honor. Just me."

"Really? Okay then, proceed."

"I'd like to call Officer Hernandez to the witness stand."

"Mr. Hernandez please take the stand."

"Mr. Pearson, you may proceed."

"Officer Hernandez, I have a white poster board on display in front of you with a picture of the intersection in question. Please look at the poster board and study the picture. Does that look like a fair representation of the corner of Twelfth Street and Main?"

"Yes it does, although the art work leaves a little to be desired (chuckle)."

"Now, Officer Hernandez, there is an "X" marked where I parked my motorcycle and then a dotted line showing the path of my motorcycle across two lanes of traffic and into the third, or right-hand lane. Does the "X" and the dotted line show where the motorcycle started and the path followed directly across Twelfth Street on the day in question?"

"Yes, it does. You started from one side, drove across the street and made the turn from the right hand lane onto Main Street. Then, I stopped you."

"So, when I turned, I had made it to the right hand lane."

"Yes, I believe so."

"Your Honor, I have no more questions."

"Okay, then. Officer Hernandez, you may step down."

"Now, Mr. Pearson, would you like to say anything in closing before I make a decision?"

"Yes, Your Honor. As the picture shows, I made the turn from the right hand lane. Under the City Code, which I have in my hand, an improper turn is described as a turn from an incorrect lane. While I may have made an improper lane change, I did not turn from an improper lane. For those reasons, I am innocent of making the improper turn as charged in the ticket."

"Well, Mr. Pearson, I can see your point. It does seem that while you were driving across traffic to get there, you did, in fact, turn from the correct lane. So, I have no choice but to let you go this time. However, I don't ever want you to do that again. Do you understand me, son?"

"Yes, Your Honor, I do."

"One more thing, Mr. Pearson. You are only seventeen, but have you thought about going to law school? If you stop representing yourself, you might have a future in the law."

"Thank you, Judge."

As I walk out of the courtroom with my poster board, Officer Hernandez looks me in the eye and says, "Nice job, kid, you're a natural. If you can drive straight, you could be a lawyer one day."

CHAPTER TWO

It is late May, after college graduation, when I finally receive the letter. I have been plucked off the end of the waiting list and offered admission into the College of Law. I later learn they expanded the class size to one hundred eighty-one students and I imagine I am the "one" after one hundred eighty of my classmates fill the law school corridors. Well, no matter. I am in and they can't take it away from me.

Once admitted, I have no idea how to prepare for law school. Alone and with no one to ask, I travel to the University bookstore and find the "Law" section. The books deal with substantive subjects for coursework. There is no "how to" book outlining the keys to survival in law school. On the bottom shelf, I find a big, thick, heavy, law dictionary. Maybe if I have one, I can look through the pages and learn some law words. That summer I learn a few Latin phrases like "res ipsa loquitor" and words with funny sounds like "fiduciary." Of course, I learn nothing of value reading portions of the dictionary on my own. Knowledge and wisdom most often require context and guidance from someone more experienced, I realize. To be fair, I did learn one thing. After starring at the back of many one-dollar bills, I looked up "e pluribus unum" written on the Great Seal of the United States.

As the August start time nears, I haven't spoken to a lawyer or an upper class law student about what law school is like or what I can do to prepare. How do I know what to do if I don't know what to do? How will I break the logjam of ignorance? I can't blindly call a law firm and ask to speak to a lawyer about law school. Even if I do, I have no time to meet and no money to go to lunch. I am consumed with work at two jobs. I spend the summer waiting tables and working at a clothing store, hoping to supplement my hourly wages with tips and commissions. If I ask for time off in the middle of a shift I will get fired.

At summer's end, I have enough money saved for books and food for the first few months of school. As my final act of preparation, I sell my motorcycle and buy a bicycle. Now, I can ride by the campus police without the nagging fear of being pulled over.

Classes start on Monday morning at nine a.m. The prior week, the freshman class, commonly called one L's, is directed to buy books and check the class assignment sheet for the first day of classes. There are cases to read and casebook chapters to review. Some classes even have problems that must be completed prior to class. Law schools use the Socratic method, which means the law professors call your name and ask you questions. I have no idea what this actually means. I imagine talking about the law will be easy. Within the first five minutes, I am quickly disabused of this notion.

My first class is contracts. Sixty eager beavers gather in an auditorium. At eight fifty-eight a.m., Professor Abrams walks briskly into the room and takes his position at the podium. He has no notes. His bow tie is neatly configured. He has the perfect professorial deportment. At the stroke of nine, he starts the interrogation of his new charges.

"Mr. Bloom, have you read the assignment?" the Professor's voice piercing the air.

"Yes, I have, Professor," Mr. Bloom responds meekly.

"Can you speak up so the class can hear you?"

"Yes, Professor," Mr. Bloom answers with more authority.

"Have you read the first case, Hawkins v. McGee?"

"Yes."

"Are you fully prepared to discuss the Hawkins case, because if you are not prepared, I will call on someone else. I do not want to embarrass you in any way."

"Thanks for the offer, but I'm prepared, Professor."

"Are you sure you're prepared?'

"Yes, I'm sure."

"Okay then, Mr. Bloom. The first word in the Hawkins case is 'assumpsit.' What does that mean?"

"I don't know."

"What do you mean you don't know?"

"I don't know."

"Mr. Bloom, I asked if you were prepared to discuss this case and you assured me you were. I even gave you the opportunity to pass and you declined."

"Well, I thought I was prepared, Professor Abrams."

"So, Mr. Bloom, let me make sure I understand. On your first class on the first day of law school, I ask you the definition of the first word in the first case and you don't even know what that is, correct?"

"Yes, that's correct. I don't know the meaning of the first word, Professor Abrams."

"Let me help you. Assumpsit is an agreement to perform an oral contract."

"Thank you, Professor Abrams."

"So, Mr. Bloom, if you assured me you were prepared and still didn't know the meaning of the first word, what would unprepared look like?"

No answer.

For the professor, this is like shooting fish in a barrel. The fish sit stunned. He smiles like a Cheshire cat.

❖

The next class is constitutional law. With even greater trepidation, sixty members of the huddled masses assemble in another auditorium classroom. I arrive fifteen minutes early and decide to sit in the front. Exactly two minutes prior to the top of the hour, Professor Lee strides in. His dress is eerily similar to Professor Abrams. He has no notes. As the second hand crosses the twelve, Professor Lee begins the interrogation.

"This class is constitutional law. Is everyone in this class prepared?"

Awkward silence.

"Is there anyone who is not prepared? If so, please raise your hand."

No one moves.

"I take it by your silence that each and every one of you is prepared for this class on constitutional law. I will start by asking one question. How many of you have read the United States Constitution in its entirety?"

No one raises his or her hand.

"Do you mean to tell me that, in preparation for your class on the Constitution, not one of you has read the Constitution? How can that be? The document outlining our principles of government was written on only four pages."

Awkward silence.

"I have another question. How many of you have heard about bankruptcy? Please raise your hand if you have heard the term bankruptcy."

Everyone slowly, reluctantly, raises his or her hand.

"Let the record reflect almost everyone raised their hand. Now, since everyone has heard of bankruptcy, does anyone in this room know where a citizen's right to bankruptcy exists?

Before you answer, let me point out I do not want you to raise your hand and offer a guess. You either know the answer or you don't. In my class, the advice attributed to Abraham Lincoln is especially appropriate: 'It is better to remain silent and be thought a fool, than to open one's mouth and remove all doubt.'"

Awkward silence.

"This is your lucky day. On the first day of class, I will provide the answer. But I will not again make this mistake."

Awkward silence.

"The answer is it is found in the Constitution. Specifically, Article I, Section eight, Clause four. The right to restructure your debts and get a fresh start in bankruptcy is so fundamental, so essential to our way of life, it is found in the Constitution itself. The founders of this country were not wealthy landowners or members of the aristocracy. This country was founded by people with the hope and dream of a better life living free from the oppressive tyranny of a few princes. They remembered a time when debtors in England who were past due on their payments could be hauled away from their families and taken to debtor's prison. Can you imagine being put in prison if you lost your job and couldn't pay your bills? What if you borrowed money to expand your business and couldn't repay because of an economic downturn, where business simply dried up. You did nothing wrong. Can you imagine the anxiety and fear you would experience as you sit in the banker's office waiting for the authorities to handcuff you and take you to jail?"

"Now, I'd like to call on someone, like I will be doing the rest of the year."

Slight pause while he checks the seating chart and then looks directly at me.

"Mr. Pearson, you are sitting in the front of class so I will call on you. Do you believe your liberty and freedom should have a price tag?"

"No, Professor Lee, I don't."

"Does the right to, and context of, bankruptcy have a new and deeper meaning to you? Is the brilliance of our four page Constitution becoming more evident?"

"Yes, Professor. I had no idea."

"As a lawyer, Mr. Pearson, are you prepared today, at this moment, to defend a citizen's rights provided under the Constitution?"

"I am not prepared to do that today, Sir, no."

Looking directly at me he says, "Then, when will you be, Mr. Pearson?"

Silence, as I had no answer.

"Class dismissed."

As I gather my belongings, I am struck by the seriousness of the question. I have no idea how quickly I will need to be ready to defend a citizen's rights. Only later do I realize the challenge issued by Professor Lee will come too quickly, almost immediately after graduation. For me, I can see the light at the end of the tunnel, but I will later discover it is a train barreling ahead. A really long freight train.

❖

On Wednesday, I attend the third class, property. The first case is the eighteen hundred five decision of Pierson v. Post in which Post and his hounds were hunting a fox but Pierson actually killed and captured the fox. Neither owned the land. Post filed suit claiming that his pursuit of the wild animal amounted to ownership. He lost, the court finding mere pursuit is not enough. Manucaption, defined as physical control, is required to establish title to personal property not connected with land or building.

Interestingly, this is the case that supports the popular phrase "possession is nine tenths of the law," when describing a person's right to personal property. If you have it, it's yours. Now I have the case authority to back it up. This is my first piece of law I think I actually might use some day. Something tangible.

❖

On Thursday at ten a.m., the one L's assemble in the main auditorium to receive our first legal writing assignment. I learn later this is the one project of law school lore experienced simultaneously by each class. We are each given the same material, a one-page description of the facts followed by nine pages filled with various types of law such as statutes, cases and rulings. We are told to write a legal memorandum not longer than five pages and it is due next Monday morning at eight a.m. sharp. We can spend as little or as much time as we think necessary but additional research is not allowed. Only the law provided can be used and it has to be our original work. No collaboration with others is permitted. It is the simplest and cruelest of assignments. Write a five page memo due Monday. Enjoy your weekend!

The law school library is buzzing for the next four days with panicked first-year law students writing and fussing from morning until night. At least half the class spends one or more "all nighters" polishing their work. I am a sleeper and will be ruined for days if I stay up. I can't understand the logic of how exhaustion will make my work product better. On Monday morning, we file in, waiting patiently in a long queue, and drop our papers off in a box in the school office. Many relieved, but none satisfied at the outcome. Then, I am off to my nine a.m. contracts class with Professor Abrams who, I am confident, is ready to terrorize us in Week Two. I am conflicted whether I am prepared for his class.

The papers are graded quickly and returned on Friday, just in time to ruin my second weekend of law school. For maximum impact, the papers are returned en mass in the same main auditorium. The legal writing professor tells us our collective effort is "about average." He also explains that, although our class is large in size, only about one hundred twenty will graduate in three years. Loudly and clearly he says, "Find two friends and look at each other. One of you will be gone." Someone raises their hand and asks with a hint of trepidation, "How many of us do you think will make it?" He responds coldly, "As many as want to."

Our names are called out and we are given our papers back along with a "key" explaining the acronyms used. The first is "B.S. means B.S." It went downhill from there. I get my paper and it is filled with red ink. I receive a fifty-eight. I am devastated. On page two, I made the astute observation that "there appears to be a certain trend" developing in the law. In big red letters, my insight is mocked with the words "as opposed to an uncertain trend?" On page three, the dreaded "B.S." is written in the margin. With the benefit of the handy "key," I know what that means. At the end of my paper, on page five, the words "Overall, not bad" are scribbled.

In the hallway, I compare notes with my classmates. The highest grade is a sixty-five and only a few are in the sixties. My fifty-eight is likely in the top third of the class. After believing I am the last one admitted, I console myself with the thought that I am making progress. I am not excelling, but I have survived the first exercise. "Not bad," has to be above bad. For me, that has to be good.

❖

By the end of the third week, the attrition is noticeable and precipitous. My guess is about thirty did not last two weeks. Many more exit quietly in week three. I am not one of them. Quitting is not an option. If I quit, I will return to my life of nothing and that is not a place I ever want to return to. Not in this lifetime. Not in the next. I fought to get in and I will fight to stay. Professor Abrams, and those like him, can shame and belittle me with their words, but they cannot break me. I simply refuse to believe otherwise.

❖

Three years hence, my class graduates one hundred twenty-five, about the number predicted. Only two-thirds of those starting want it bad enough to finish and earn a juris doctor degree. I am one of them. I am not at the top of the class, but I am not at the bottom, either. I have successfully turned "not bad" into good. Like a marathon runner needing to post a minimum qualifying time, I make it to the race. Fear is a powerful motivator. But how long will it burn inside? When will fear subside and normal take its place?

CHAPTER THREE

After one day spent settling in at the mid-level corporate law firm of Dewey, Frederick and Carlyle, I am jolted into my new reality when I receive an interoffice phone call from my supervising attorney, Lou Stevens.

I pick up the telephone handset for the first time and say, "Hello, Jeff Pearson here."

"Jeff, I'd like you to come into my office ASAP. Bring your legal pad."

"Yes, Lou. I'm in the middle of a writing project for another lawyer, but I'll be there in a few minutes."

"Don't tell me your problems. Hurry." I drop the handset into the cradle like it's hot.

I arrive in Lou's office while he is finishing a call. He motions for me to sit down on one of his red leather client chairs facing his large hand-carved mahogany desk and indicates by holding his index and thumb finger close together that he will only be a few minutes. Gazing up on his office wall, I notice his degrees are written in Latin. This is logical, since Lou graduated from Yale University with a degree in European history and Yale Law School. He wears ties with heraldic shields and little bulldogs on them often tied not so neatly underneath the collar of a blue button down oxford shirt. I can only assume those are not garden-variety bulldogs, but ones of the special Yale variety. He even has a "Handsome Dan" iron bulldog on his credenza. Being a trial lawyer, he enjoys verbal jousting with the other lawyers in the firm while reminding them he is the only one from an Ivy League school. Rumor has it he is at this mid-level firm for some odd reason, that all is not perfect in paradise, but I have not heard the explanation. Clearly, he is out of place.

He ends his call and turns his considerable gaze to me. I have my pen and paper ready for furious note taking.

In his deep trial voice he says, "Jeff, the law firm is on a pro bono list for complex cases maintained by the city bar association. We have special expertise and, as a part of our duty as lawyers, we make that expertise available where the client's legal needs are complicated, but they can't afford to pay the freight. You will be amazed that ordinary people can have some really complex and vexing legal problems."

I nod in recognition not in understanding.

"We haven't had one of these cases in a few years, but I received a call from the head of the city bar advising that a Maria DeMore would be calling. I just spoke to her and she really sounds panicked. She wants to meet immediately after lunch at one p.m., but I have a hearing this afternoon. So, I told her you would meet her to discuss her problem and get the facts."

"So, I don't need to do anything, just meet her and get her to explain her situation?"

"Yes, that's right. You're the new guy without any other client demands or deadlines to get in the way and this type of case will get you some immediate client contact. She has no expectations of experience level and will be happy to meet any one here. To her, a lawyer is a lawyer and any one will do."

"Okay. I can do that and then I'll report back to you later."

"Fine. Also, you need to reserve Conference Room A if you can get it and let the receptionist know where to send Ms. DeMore when she arrives."

"Will do. I will handle it."

At one p.m., I walk into Conference Room A and see a pleasant looking woman of about thirty-five, average build, with short hair slightly bobbed and sprayed in place. She looks like she has made an effort to put on her church clothes. She is sitting at attention, back perfectly straight, with two hands tightly clutching a small purse she holds in front of her. She is normal and suburban in every way, except for her bloodshot, nervous and darting eyes. They tell a different story.

"Are you Ms. DeMore?"

"Yes, I am," she says softly, as she stands up to greet me.

"Nice to meet you. My name is Jeff Pearson, and I am the attorney assigned to meet you and discuss your legal problems. Here is my business card with my contact information," I say as I place my card on the table in front of her. "Please sit down. Would you like some water?"

"Yes, and some tissues too, if you have them."

I walk out of the conference room and get a box of tissues from a secretarial station and water from the break area. I return and sit down in the chair opposite hers on the other side of the large conference table.

I place my hands on the table and in a kind voice say, "So, tell me Ms. DeMore, what kind of a legal issue do you have and how can I help you?"

"Well, I just met you and you're a stranger, so I don't know what to say, exactly."

"Ms. DeMore, I'm a lawyer and you can tell me what sort of legal problem you have. Then, we can go from there."

"It's not that simple."

"Okay, then, I'll be more direct. When did you realize you had a legal problem?"

"When the FBI agent and two IRS agents showed up at my door."

"What did you just say?"

"I said I realized I had a problem when the three agents flashing badges showed up at my house yesterday."

"What did they say?"

"They asked to see my husband, Barry, and I told them he was not home. He travels a lot for work and he wasn't home. They asked if I'd seen or heard from him lately and I said not since Monday when he left for his business trip. I then asked them what was the matter?"

"What did they tell you?"

"They said my husband was a thief."

"Is that really what they said? What were their exact words?"

"The FBI agent said my husband was involved in a large scheme at his company and he had taken a lot of money that didn't belong to him. He works for the Western Horizon Cable Company but never has had a problem. One of the IRS agents handed me a letter saying that Barry and I together owe back taxes on the stolen money. She asked me if I knew anything about this and I said no, this was news to me. Then, she said I needed to find a good lawyer because I was going to need one. I asked her why I needed a lawyer when I didn't do anything wrong and didn't even know about this. She said because when you are married you both owe taxes for all earnings, even if the money is stolen. I burst out in tears and they left."

"Do you have the letter?"

"Yes, I have it in my purse. Here it is," she says as she pulls it out and hands the envelope to me.

I open the envelope and quickly read the letter with the words "Internal Revenue Service" engraved in bold across the top. This is official government business on official letterhead.

I look up and say, "Based on a quick reading, the letter says the IRS has reconstructed your earnings based on new information and you and your husband jointly owe roughly twenty million dollars in back taxes, interest and penalties."

"I can't believe it. This is a nightmare (sobbing). This is not real."

"Did the IRS lady who handed the letter to you give you her business card?"

"Yes, she did and I threw it in the trash."

"Have you heard from your husband, Barry?"

"No, I've called and he doesn't answer. His voice mailbox is full and not taking messages. We have problems like everyone, but he's a good man and would never do this. He's my husband. He's the cub master for our kids and there's a den meeting tomorrow evening. They have to tie ropes and he was getting the different ropes ready. I know he will show up. He never misses a den meeting. He doesn't make a late payment on his credit card. He doesn't even speed in his car. He sits at the kid's soccer games on the weekends talking on his cell phone, but always waives to our kids. He cheers when they score a goal. They have a soccer game this weekend."

"How many kids do you have?"

"Two boys, Michael eight and Randall six. I have their school photos in my wallet."

"Anything else you can tell me?"

"Barry would never take money. He has a savings account. He has a coin collection. He would never do this. They've mistaken my Barry for someone else, I know it. That's what this is, mistaken identity, like on one of those TV shows."

"Thanks Ms. DeMore. I'll check with one of the other lawyers here and get back to you."

"Please help me. You're the only lawyer I know. This can't be real. Make it stop."

I hand her a piece of blank notepaper and say, "Please write your phone number down on this paper and I will get back to you."

She scribbles her number and pushes the paper back towards me.

"Did you drive here? What kind of car do you drive?"

"I drive a six year-old minivan. It needs new tires and pulls to the right. I need to clean out the food wrappers. The kids pull the door handles too hard."

"Okay, that will do it for now. Let me escort you out to the reception area so you can be on your way," I say as we both get up and prepare to walk out.

We walk out.

As she leaves, I'm worried about her stressful condition and say in a caring tone, "Please drive carefully."

I turn around and start walking back to my office. Maria's story seems like a problem between the IRS and her husband. Whatever he did he must answer for, but it clearly doesn't involve her. As she explained, it looks to be a big misunderstanding. Why should she be made to suffer any more than she already is? Surely, I can get this resolved if I can meet with the IRS folks in person. I cannot believe the enormous sense of injustice. How dare they knock on her door and demand twenty million dollars in back taxes.

I enter my office and sit down to contemplate what just happened. In my first week of law school, Professor Lee asked me when I would be ready to defend a citizen. I had no idea it would be this quickly, but this is why I became a lawyer in the first place. If I don't right this wrong, nobody will. Fortunately, this should not take too long to get straightened out. Facts clear, results clear. I have logic and justice on my side. Logic surely will prevail. This is obviously not her tax problem. A misunderstanding that just needs to be cleared up.

CHAPTER FOUR

The next morning, I knock on Lou's office door, open it slowly and take one step into his office and say, "Am I interrupting anything?" Lou looks up from the papers on his desk and stares directly at me and says, "You are now." I chuckle at the clever word play, while his face remains solemn. He has the reputation for being hard on associates. He does not mince words nor use many of them. I nervously walk over and sit down on the edge of the same red leather chair and start in.

"Lou, I met with Maria DeMore yesterday and I'd like to give you a report."

"Proceed," he says as he sits up in his chair and begins to rock nervously.

"An FBI agent and two IRS agents showed up at Maria's house yesterday. The FBI agent asked if her husband, Barry, was home and when told he was not, advised Maria that Barry is under investigation for embezzling money from the Western Horizon Cable Company where he works."

"What did she say in response?"

"She is totally shocked by the allegations and said it's not believable. According to her, he is a good man and would never do something like this. She swears they have him confused with someone else."

"Where's the husband, Barry?"

"Ms. DeMore hasn't seen him since Monday and he hasn't returned her calls. He's dropped out of sight."

"What did the IRS agents say?"

“The IRS agents said the money taken by Barry in this scheme is taxable to both Barry and Maria because they are married. One of the agents gave Ms. DeMore a letter saying the IRS has reconstructed their income and adjusted it up, way up. The agent told Maria she needed a good lawyer which is why she came to see us for help.”

“How far is up? How much does the IRS say they owe now?”

“If you add up the taxes, interest and fraud penalties, the total is almost twenty million dollars.”

“That sounds like ridiculous money, but the IRS tends to make the numbers high when you first get into these types of cases. They throw the mud on the wall and see what sticks. Pretty common and I’m not surprised. What’s Maria’s reaction?”

“Stunned. Angry. Complete disbelief. She says this is a case of mistaken identity, like one of those shows on TV. She’s distraught at the severity of the crimes alleged against her husband, but then defending him at the same time.”

“Do you believe she had anything to do with it?”

“I’m convinced she didn’t.”

“Based on what evidence? Your gut feeling? How long have you been practicing law, a week? So, based on a week’s worth of experience you’re ready to announce your gut feeling to the world and then rely on it without anything more. What’s wrong with you?”

“Sorry, Lou, but I don’t believe she was involved.”

“Jeff, you are really wasting oxygen here by expressing your words of conviction. A good lawyer will look at it from the opposite perspective. Believe nothing and trust no one are the first words to live by. The fact is you don’t know squat.”

“Well, I did ask her what kind of car she drives and she tells me it’s a six year-old minivan that needs new tires.”

“A slight improvement over the zero facts you had just a minute earlier.”

“So, what are we going to do next, Lou?”

"What do you mean *we*? There is no *we* here. I'm working on another case and under deadline. There is only you and you need to keep working the case and find more facts than the one you have so far."

"How do I do that?"

Exasperated, he says, "Well, Sherlock, didn't they teach you anything in law school? Do I need to call your Dean and ask for a refund? It seems like an education is so often wasted on the young."

I stare at Lou in complete bewilderment. I can't move, wondering what to do next.

Sensing weakness and on a roll, Lou continues and says, "Cases start with facts. You need to immediately start the fact-finding process. Go out and ask my secretary to give you the names and numbers of three different private investigation firms. Call them up and see if they will help you on the case. You're really behind the eight ball on this one."

"Thanks. When should I report back?"

"When you actually know something? Now, get out of my office."

I immediately get up and run for the door.

In the afternoon, I attend my first State Bar ethics program. Even though I am newly admitted to the bar as a practicing lawyer, I am obligated to meet the annual mandatory ethics study requirement.

For the first half of the program, humorless officials from the State Bar explain a lawyer's obligation to get fee agreements in writing and maintain a trust account for any client money deposited with you. Then, they emphasize the general duties of timeliness and civility, with examples. The other lawyers in the room laugh nervously when the subject of civility is mentioned. I am slightly confused because, being from the Midwest, I think everyone will be civil and behave appropriately with professional decorum.

While the first half of the program is not surprising, the second half shocks me. The topic is substance abuse. How to recognize it, how to treat it and how to report it if you see it in others. I naively think since lawyers are trained professionals subject to standards of ethics; this will not be a big problem and certainly not one worthy of hours of discussion. They present the findings of a recent study showing the problem to be pervasive, bordering on epidemic. This is reality, not theory.

At the conclusion of the program, a State Bar official hands out a glossy flyer with two different eight hundred numbers. One I can call for ethics questions and the second one I can dial to report others or myself for substance abuse. With youthful ignorance firmly planted, I doubt this will apply in my world. I will not let the pressure get to me and I surely will not be practicing with a lawyer with a substance abuse problem. I toss the flyer in the recycle bin on the way out.

CHAPTER FIVE

I arrive in my office the next morning and get organized for the task at hand. At nine a.m. I start dialing the numbers Lou's secretary gave me. I leave messages at the first two private investigation firms. "Hello, this is Jeff Pearson, attorney with the law firm of Dewey, Frederick and Carlyle, and I'd like to speak to you about your investigation services." My phone messaging abilities are weak to say the least and I practice my speech before making the third call. How do I talk on the phone if I've never talked on the phone? Since I am new, everything I do seems like it is for the first time. After practicing with no one on the other end of the line, I feel like I might be conquering phone messaging. One task down, how many thousand more to go?

The third number belongs to Watershed Investigations. I call and reach a live person who announces, "Watershed Investigations, how may I help you?" I say I am a lawyer with the Dewey, Frederick law firm and I would like to speak to an investigator about their services. "Just a minute," and she puts me on hold. Their elevator music is particularly annoying and I am expecting this to be a rough and tumble conversation. I ready my pen and yellow legal pad.

The confident, professional, mellifluous, voice I am connected with catches me by complete surprise.

"Allison speaking. How may I help you?"

"Hi," stumbling slightly, "this is Jeff Pearson and I'm a lawyer with the Dewey, Frederick law firm and I'd like to speak with you about investigation services."

"How did you get our name and number?"

"I got your number from another lawyer here, Lou Stevens."

"Let me check. I need to put you on hold."

I wait on hold for a few minutes.

"Okay, I see his name with Dewey Frederick in our database. All right, we can talk. We always have to be cautious about conflicts and make sure we don't speak to someone on the other side of a case. What type of investigation are you looking for?"

"Well, I don't know exactly. What services do you offer?"

"Let me ask it differently. What type of case are you working on?"

"It's difficult to explain, but I'll try. We ... I ... have been appointed to represent an innocent spouse."

"They all are, aren't they?"

We both chuckle at the thought.

"I hadn't looked at that way. Anyway, my ... our client's husband is being accused of embezzling large sums of money from his company. But that's not the worst of it. Even though my client is innocent and has nothing to do with the scheme, the IRS is saying she is liable for back taxes on the total amount stolen because they are married and file joint returns."

"So, do you mean the IRS is trying to stick her with the back taxes for the money her husband stole?"

"Yup, that sums it up."

"That's rotten."

"That is exactly how she feels. She sobbed uncontrollably when she told me her story."

"Jeff, do you think you can win this case? This is intense. What are you going to do?"

"She's alone, her husband is missing, she's got two small kids and to top it off she gets a bill from the IRS hand delivered at her front door for her husband's criminal actions. I can't turn my back on her."

"This is the worst of the worst. I have never heard of a woman's life turning to crap so quickly."

"So, will you help me?"

"Well, our normal services include such things as locating and interviewing witnesses, gathering evidence, reviewing and assessing government evidence and using the Internet to find out information. I guess all of that applies to your case."

"Yes, I'm going to need all of those services. The FBI is alleging the husband is the ringleader of a massive fraud and the IRS is following along and charging back taxes on the money. I've got a lot of evidence to review in order to figure out whether the facts are true and whether she has any defenses. I'm starting at square one."

"Where's the husband, have you been able to talk to him?"

"No, he's been missing since Monday."

"Surprise, surprise. Well, I don't have a particular expertise, but we do have former FBI agents and forensic investigators here at Watershed and maybe they can help."

"Exactly the kind of expertise I need."

"But, before I commit to anything, I need to check with the head of the agency. Every once in a while, the agency agrees to take on a case for the underdog who's being framed by the system and this one certainly qualifies under that category."

"Thanks for your time, Allison. Please check and get back to me as soon as you can."

"I will. Keep your fingers crossed."

Being "the new guy" at the firm, I am the instant target of the older associates. If this were torts class, I would be an "attractive nuisance." After returning from lunch, I walk through the front door and the receptionist announces loudly, "Jeff, you have a phone message from a Mr. Lyon. It sounds urgent and he wants you to call him immediately." Confirming we are transacting official business, she hands me a formal paper phone message with "Mr. Lyon" as the caller and the phone number filled in. The message is even signed by the receptionist with the time noted prominently.

When I reach my tiny office, I'm excited to put my new phone skills to good use. I promptly dial the number and, without hesitating, confidently announce I am returning Mr. Lyon's call and I would like to speak to him immediately, as he indicated the matter to be urgent. Without missing a beat, the voice on the other end of the phone says, "This is the City Zoo and Mr. Lion will not be able to speak with you now or likely ever!" To my credit, having been fooled once, I did not return the other phone messages left for me from Elsie (the cow at the dairy) or Jack (from the fast food restaurant bearing his name).

In the afternoon, I repeatedly stop by Lou's office but he is not around. Searching through the entire firm, I find his secretary at the copy machine.

"Hi Betty. I'm looking for Lou."

"He's deep into the new securities case that just came in the door and he's meeting with clients."

"I want to give him an update on the Maria DeMore matter and tell him I reached someone at Watershed Investigations."

"He doesn't have time for you now, Jeff. You need to keep the DeMore matter moving forward as best you can. Lou can pick it up later. Just keep it going."

"Okay."

CHAPTER SIX

I stop by my favorite coffee shop on the way to the office. I order a blended Americano and the local newspaper. I sit down and bury my head in the morning edition. Work stress is different than law school stress, I am slowly realizing, and reading the paper calms me down. With new habits forming quickly, I have a paper-reading pattern. I always start with the daily chuckle on the inside of the front page, which today is dumb, and then read the daily prayer. I am struck by the powerful simplicity of today's prayer: "Lord, grant me strength and wisdom." That is it. Nothing more. My thoughts linger as the words sink in. I see the mattress ads glaring and I am ready to turn the page. But something holds me back.

After the message sinks in a little deeper, I turn the pages quickly thru the first two sections. Pictures and ads seem to dominate. Leading the frugal life of a new lawyer, I don't need what they are selling. Everything offered seems to match and nothing I own does. Maybe someday that will change. Looking down at my feet, what I need are new shoes. But that money hasn't been earned yet.

I pull out the business section, and my eyes lock onto a small headline in the right-hand column: "Cable Executive Charged." I am riveted by the words. The article begins with impact. An executive with the Western Horizon Cable Company has been charged in a criminal complaint with multiple counts of fraud and embezzlement, as the result of a six-month investigation by the FBI. The executive, Barry DeMore, has been missing since Monday and is still at-large. His co-conspirators named in the complaint, Scott Peters and Logan Wilborn, worked for two companies supplying Western Horizon with new fiber optic cable and other products. They were arrested and arraigned on similar charges yesterday. Western Horizon, a prominent public company, has launched an internal investigation to uncover the facts of the scandal and vowed to bring those responsible to justice. "We are shocked and saddened by the events of today. We commit to our shareholders and stakeholders that we will undertake a thorough investigation to find out what happened," says Bill Bradley, President and CEO of Western Horizon. "While there are significant dollars allegedly involved, we believe this to be limited to a division within the purchasing department headed by Mr. DeMore," he continued. "We will release further details as they become available." Western's stock declined, in active trading.

I hurriedly grab the business section, get up and rush out the door. A customer at the coffee shop yells, "Hey buddy, you forgot your coffee and bagel!" I would have worried about that twenty seconds ago, but my life just changed in a flash. Food was previously important, but no longer. I turn briefly to acknowledge with a wave of the hand and then clutching the paper ever tighter, I run. Confused thoughts are rushing through my mind. I never have known someone mentioned in the paper, much less one allegedly involved as a central figure in a crime. This is too overwhelming. Blood rushes to my head. I feel flushed. This is real.

❖

Out of breath, I open Lou's door without knocking and walk briskly into his office. He is on a call and waives me off with his hand. I sit down in his red office chair and try to calm myself down and organize my thoughts. How do I explain this one? At least I had the paper crushed in my hand as demonstrativc evidence.

"What do you want, Jeff. I'm busy and I asked you not to bother me until you gathered the facts."

"Lou, I have facts you won't believe. Barry DeMore has been indicted. Here is the morning paper with the story."

"Let me look at that," he says as he grabs the crumpled paper from my hand. He takes a moment and studies the story carefully.

Looking up from the paper, he says, "You need to get a copy of the criminal complaint. Call the PI firm you are working with, Watershed, and ask them to get a copy of the complaint. That should detail the allegations and describe the factual basis for the complaint."

"Okay, will do."

"Have you spoken to Ms. DeMore since this story broke?"

"No, but I will call her right after I speak to Allison at Watershed and confirm they're on board."

I return to my office, get a blue pen and position my yellow legal notepad near the phone for legal note taking. I dial Allison's number.

"Watershed Investigations. How may I direct your call?"

"I'd like to speak with Allison Broadmore, please."

"One moment. I'll see if she's available."

I'm placed on hold with annoying background elevator music. If I have the chance, I will one day advise Allison of the deleterious affect the music has on my ears.

"This is Allison. How can I help you?"

"Hey, Allison, this is Jeff Pearson at the DFC law firm calling. How are you?"

"Hello, Jeff. I'm fine. How are you?"

"Not so great. Did you see the headline in the paper this morning? It is a front-page headline and detailed story. Maria's husband, Barry DeMore, has been indicted."

"Shut up! Are you serious?"

"As serious as a heart attack. Did you get clearance from the head of your agency to work on this case?"

"Sorry I didn't back to you sooner. Things have been a little hectic around here. Good news, with a little persuading from yours truly, I got the agency to agree to help. We're on a limited budget, so we can't do full field surveillance or extensive forensic work, but we can help you with the rest."

"That's awesome. Maria desperately needs help and I've got to win this thing."

"Do you really think you can win, Jeff? This has got loser written all over it."

"I don't have any choice. If I don't win, Maria and her kids will be stuck with these taxes for the rest of their lives. The odds don't matter. I'm driven to find a way to win."

"I admire your attitude. I don't think many lawyers would take on this battle against the IRS. They usually just crush people and move on. They are like a D9 mining bulldozer."

"How do you know about a D9 bulldozer?"

"I loved to watch the shows about heavy construction equipment when I was a little girl. Instead of playing house, I would play in the dirt. I wanted trucks instead of dolls. I like to do things rather than just play imaginary games. I drove my parents crazy."

"You're amazing. Now, on the case, can you find the criminal complaint document and get a copy. Is that possible?"

"Sure, we do it all the time. There should also be a sworn affidavit from the investigating FBI agent, which I will try to find as well. I will fax it over to you as soon as I get it."

"Many thanks, Allison. I'll get back to you with next steps. Now, I need to call Ms. DeMore and tell her we are on the case. If she wants to meet in person, is your calendar open for the next few days?"

"Yes, I can make time and your office is not far away."

"I'll keep you posted."

"Good luck. You're going to need all of it and more, I'm afraid."

I dial the phone number Maria DeMore wrote down on the sheet of paper and an inaudible voice answers.

"Ms. DeMore, is that you?

"Yes," she responds softly

"Ms. DeMore, this is Jeff Pearson at the Dewey, Frederick law firm. Do you have time to talk?"

"Yes," sniffling.

"Ms. DeMore, I saw the article in the paper this morning about your husband, Barry, and I'm so sorry. Are you Okay?"

"Not really. It's been a nightmare that keeps getting worse. I want it to go away. I had to take the kids to school and act like nothing is happening in front of them but they know something bad is going on."

"I'm sorry you have to go through this."

"Not half as sorry as I am, Mr. Pearson."

"Have you seen or heard from your husband, Barry?"

"No, I haven't. My kids keep asking and I don't know what to say. My phone has been ringing off the hook with every crazy person calling. It's like I've been dropped on a strange planet and everything's wrong. I tried to tie the ropes at the Cub Scout meeting, but I am hopeless. The car needs gas."

"Please don't talk to the callers."

"That's easy. I don't and just slam the phone down. I hope I don't break it."

"Ms. DeMore, I will represent you in the fight against the IRS. I believe that, if I can talk to somebody there, a real person, I think they will listen to reason."

"That would be a first."

"I need help investigating the background of the case and Allison Broadmore at Watershed Investigations has agreed to help. I'd like to meet with you and Ms. Broadmore at my office next Tuesday at say ten a.m. Can you make it then?"

"Next Tuesday at ten in your same office? Yes, I'll be there."

"Thanks, Ms. DeMore. I'll see you then."

"Sure," she says as her soft voice trails off.

CHAPTER SEVEN

I am in my office early Monday morning and receive a call from Allison at Watershed Investigations.

"Jeff Pearson speaking."

"Jeff, this is Allison at Watershed. Do you have a minute?"

"I have all day for you, Allison. What have you got?"

"We found the criminal complaint against Barry DeMore and two co-conspirators. The complaint is signed and sworn to by Jack Ledington, an FBI special agent, before a United States Magistrate Judge. A twenty-one-page affidavit is attached, detailing the investigation. Special Agent Ledington is the primary case agent responsible for the investigation of Mr. DeMore. He specializes in white-collar crimes, including embezzlement, wire fraud, money laundering and various other types of financial misdeeds. My former FBI colleagues here know of Special Agent Ledington and this is not his first rodeo. Barry DeMore is toast."

"What do you mean he's toast?"

"Special Agent Ledington is thorough and meticulous. Based on a six-month investigation, he has outlined an unbelievable story involving Barry and his two buddies. Through a complex web of entities, contracts, off-setting book entries and schemes coordinated by using the phases of the moon, they defalcated, stole in layman's terms, over fifty million dollars. The FBI agent does admit the amount is approximate, but reliable."

"This sounds too unbelievable to be true about the Barry DeMore described by his wife."

"He obviously led a double life of crime."

"What should we do now?"

"I planned to fax whatever we found to your office. But this is too complex. We need to meet in person and I need to explain it to you. There is a lot of FBI jargon in the report that needs to be explained so you can understand. I can be there in an hour."

"Sounds good. This is beyond my ability to comprehend. In the Midwest, people only live one life at a time, not two. But you're more experienced in this stuff and I'm sure your explanation will help me get a grip on this."

"I have your law firm's address. See you in an hour."

I call the receptionist and reserve Conference Room A. After I hang up, I pause for a moment to inventory my capabilities; I can talk on the phone and find a place to talk in person. My talking skills are progressing nicely. If only my lawyering skills could follow the same upward trajectory. I call Lou's secretary, Betty, and ask her to tell Lou we have a meeting that afternoon with Allison and invite Lou to attend. Judging from Betty's nonresponse, I assume I am going alone.

I receive an interoffice call from the receptionist. "Ms. Broadmore is here to see you," she says.

I walk into the reception area and find Allison waiting. Our eyes lock with instant, matched, intensity, like those of two knowing souls connecting at a deeper level. I have a hard time forming words. Her looks are captivating, paring perfectly with her mellifluous voice. Her stylish, professionally coiffed, light brown hair glistens and her bright eyes radiate warmth, beauty and intelligence. Her dress is impeccable and stands out as that rare blend of stylish and high-end professional. She is wearing a tan skirt and matching short-length jacket with a blouse tying in a scarf-like knot at the top. Her jacket has intricate detailed stitching on the collar and sleeves. It looks like her sleeve buttons actually function and are not simply sewn on the top of the fabric. Her tailored clothes fit her perfectly. Like her, it appears, there is a lot more depth and detail on closer inspection. She is a private eye with more than meets the eye.

Gently shaking myself back to reality, I have to break the trance and speak or I'll melt like ice cream in the desert.

"Nice to finally meet you, Allison," I stammer like a schoolboy.

"Nice to meet you too, Jeff," her words flowing with confident authority and grace.

"I have Conference Room A reserved for the balance of the afternoon. It's down the hall to the right. Would you like some water?"

"Yes, water would be good."

We make our way to the conference room and sit down at the end of the long table, opposite each other. Her looks are patently distracting to me. I am confident she does not share my problem.

Wasting no time, she says, "Let's get started, Jeff," with the efficiency of an experienced investigator. "Here's the copy of the criminal complaint and the sworn affidavit," she says as she hands a large envelope filled with papers to me.

I open the envelope, remove the papers and look at the dense detail on the first page.

"Before you start reading, let me explain how this works. The FBI's financial fraud unit is filled with lawyers, CPA's and computer experts who are very intelligent and highly trained. Special Agent Ledington has led a six-month investigation of Barry DeMore and his pals using the latest information-gathering techniques of surveillance, wiretapping and eavesdropping. You name it, they've done it. After gathering the hard data, including phone records, bank records and computer records, likely obtained directly from the source with subpoenas, Agent Ledington has used a battalion of experts to put the puzzle together. They miss nothing. Also, you can tell from the detail that at least one of the other co-conspirators has turned state's evidence and is a cooperating witness. In FBI jargon, this is called 'flipping the witness.'

If this were the Olympic gymnastics of fraud investigation, they would score a perfect ten, even from the Eastern Bloc judge."

"Where I grew up we flipped pancakes. That's a joke. Proceed. I'm listening."

"I've reviewed the twenty-page fact-finding affidavit and I'm going to tell you a story that seems to be a work of fiction. The only problem for us is, it's virtually certain to be true. These FBI guys just don't run around the country making stuff up and their conviction rate is really high."

"Go on."

"Barry's scheme started when the three amigos met at a cable industry conference four years ago. The industry is in the midst of a historic shift from hard cable to fiber optic cable. This requires a massive spend by the cable companies. Basically, these three set up a dummy Delaware limited liability company; I'll call it Skimco, to act as the intermediary. The other two would each get their companies to sell new fiber optic cable to Skimco, which would, in turn, re-sell at a higher price to Western Horizon. The profit, or juice, would be left in Skimco. Barry, as the purchasing manager at Western Horizon, was the ringleader and made payments out to the other two from Skimco. The scheme was actually more complex with financing arrangements, double bill to, bill from, accounts set up inside Western Horizon, and the timing of the actions coordinated without any paper trail or phone calls using the phases of the moon. Bottom line, for the past three years the stolen money was collected by Skimco. Any questions so far?"

"No, please continue."

"The scheme started small but quickly grew large and out of hand. Their interactions became more elaborate, with secret meetings, the exchange of envelopes, drop offs of computer flash drives and communicating via coffeehouse Wi-Fi connections. I believe the FBI has video. To hide the proceeds, Skimco set up a series of off-shore Bahamian bank accounts which are difficult to track."

"I'm speechless. This is difficult for me to wrap my head around."

"I can understand and it's a lot to bite off and chew on. Our investigation has just begun and I'll have more to report to you. But, I wanted to give you the storyline so far based on the publicly available documents. There is a lot more work we need to do to complete the story."

"The IRS is saying Barry stole the money and it's taxable income to both Barry and Maria. Any defenses jump out at you from what you've seen?"

"Interesting question. Most lawyers just assume they know it all and don't ask that question. Sometimes, I do uncover some kind of defense, but this would not be one of those cases. The acronym WYSIWYG applies so far. I'm sorry I can't reward your great question with a great answer."

"Thanks," I say with a sigh of resignation. "While you investigate and uncover the facts, I've got to figure out how to win this thing."

"Understand we've got different roles here. I'm going to leave and get back to my office."

"Remember, we have our meeting with Maria DeMore here tomorrow at ten a.m. Same Conference Room A."

"Thanks. See you then," she says as we both get up and gather our papers.

"I'll walk you out," I say as I follow her out of the conference room and down the hall.

Looking down, her shoes are stylish and professional, with a color perfectly matching her suit. Mine are scuffed. I look like crap. Memo to self: get one good pair of lawyer shoes for your new day job. Get a credit card and charge them if you must.

I return to my office and slump in my chair, tired and depressed. I have not heard a response from Lou or Lou's secretary, Betty, to my message left earlier. Lonely could not even begin to describe it. Silence is not golden. I am feeling the pressure mount, much like I imagine an unpublished college professor who must "publish or perish" feels when approaching next year's deadline for tenure. While the pursuit may be academic, the human feelings are real. Real bad for me.

Rather than continue the self-created pity-party, I start reviewing the criminal complaint document provided by Allison, in preparation for my meeting with Maria DeMore tomorrow. The intensity level is ratcheting up. This is not a memorandum to the file I am reading. This is an FBI report meticulously prepared by a team of FBI agents. This is a page-turner of epic proportions. This *is* a federal case. My self-pity returns almost immediately. I put my head in my hands. Is there crying in the law?

CHAPTER EIGHT

At nine forty-five a.m. I receive a call from the receptionist that Maria DeMore has arrived. I walk into the reception room and see Maria wiping her eyes. She has been crying. Her hair is sprayed in place and she is wearing different dress clothes. She looks and appears put together until I see her face. Dilated eyes a radiant, misty red and wrinkles in her forehead tell the story of a woman under siege.

Shaking slightly, she hands an aluminum foil covered plate to me and says "Mr. Pearson, I can't pay you money, but I baked these cookies for you. These are my special oatmeal chocolate chip with cinnamon and nutmeg. My kids love them and I had to shoe them away so they wouldn't eat these." Touched by her gesture in the midst of total chaos, I say, "Thank you so much, Ms. DeMore. I love chocolate chip cookies and I will share them with the staff. You are very thoughtful." Then, I escort her to the conference room. Remembering her preference, I have already positioned a glass of water and a full box of tissues on the table.

After making small talk, Allison walks in and takes a seat a few chairs over on Maria's side of the table. I apprehensively start the meeting, knowing the conversation is going to be difficult and emotionally treacherous. My mouth is dry, making it hard to form my words.

"Ms. DeMore, I'd like to introduce you to Allison Broadmore who works for Watershed Investigations. We need to dig into and uncover the facts of your case and Allison has agreed to help."

"Thank you, Ms. Broadmore for helping me. I'm in quite a mess."

"Now, Ms. DeMore, have you heard from or had any contact with Barry?"

"No, and something's really wrong. The police have been at my house looking for him and I'm worried sick. They mentioned the words foul play, but I don't understand. He missed the Cub Scout meeting and the kids' soccer. Everybody's asking where's Barry. That's so not like him. Even when he traveled a lot, he still made it home. I keep thinking he'll just walk through the door. I just want him back," she says, sobbing.

"I'm so sorry, Ms. DeMore. My prayers are with you and your family."

She takes a drink of water and pulls a fresh tissue out of the box.

"Have you heard about the charges filed against your husband?"

"Yes, the commotion started almost immediately. I don't know what to believe. They've got him confused with someone else. It's not him and I just want him home."

"Do you know anything about this, Ms. DeMore?"

"No, not a clue. Honest. I just live my life in my house and try to take care of the boys. I still believe he has a job at the cable company and he just works there. He travels a lot and comes home on the weekends. He does not want to talk about work. He gets moody, but so does everybody. We never have much money, but we make ends meet."

"So, you could take the witness stand and swear you didn't know and weren't involved?"

"Absolutely. I'm in the dark and it looks like I am in the dark about a lot of things."

"Would you be willing to sign a sworn statement as well?"

"Yes, I didn't do anything wrong," sobbing as she wiped her eyes. "I have problems but not these ones."

"Have you dramatically changed your lifestyle in the past two years. Taken any big trips. Bought any jewelry?"

"We went to Disneyland with the kids, does that count? I have my wedding ring and my grandmother's necklace. Other than what I can think of, nothing's really changed. I'm sorry I can't do better, my mind is so confused."

"Is there anything you would like to say to me?"

"Yes," she says a little surprised at the question. "I got another letter from the IRS in the mail and I saved it in my purse to bring it to you. Here it is," she says as she opens her purse, grabs it and hands an official-looking IRS envelope to me.

"Thanks," I say as I place the envelope on the table in front of me. "With your permission, I'll open it later."

"Yes, of course. You're my lawyer. I told you before the other two lawyers would not take my case, would not help me."

"Now, I need you to sign some documents," I say as I place the documents on the table in front of her. "The first is a client representation letter which says I will be your lawyer and the second is a power of attorney form which allows me to represent you before the IRS."

"A power of what form?"

"A power of attorney form from the IRS. They won't let me talk to them or get information from them about you without getting your signature right here at the bottom."

"Okay. I'll sign."

"Please sign and date there," I say pointing to the signature line.

She signs.

"Will you talk to them, explain my situation?"

"That's what I'm going to try to do."

"Make it go away."

"Now, the next steps are Ms. Broadmore will be doing some investigation to try and figure out what happened. She will meet you at your house and talk to your neighbors. Is that Okay?"

"Yes, sure. There are no secrets now."

"She will call you to set up a convenient time in the next few days. Anything else come to mind?"

"I want my life back, Jeff. Tell them to stop."

"I will try, I will try," I say as we both get up and start to walk out.

"Now, let me escort you out and have a good rest of your day," I say as we walk down the hallway and she leaves the office.

I return to the conference room, walk in and take a seat directly across from Allison.

"Well, what do you think? You are far more experienced at this stuff than I am."

"She's obviously a distraught woman who's facing the loss of her husband and the destruction of her life as she knew it. When you think about the magnitude of it all, she is holding up amazingly well. She is not what I expected, but I didn't know what to expect, oddly."

"Do you believe her story?"

"That's always a difficult question because there's so much pain that could be used to mask other facts. That being said, and in my business you have to say it that way because my job is to be skeptical of everything and everyone, I do not see any obvious signs of deception. I want to follow through and meet her in her home and visit with her neighbors, but at this moment, I can't see how she would know and, even if she had an inkling, how she might have benefited. It just does not add up. I guess that's a long-winded way of saying yes I believe her story. I'll be shocked if I find anything out about her to contradict it."

"Thanks for your thoughtful words and professional opinion. Maria DeMore is lucky to have you on her side."

"Lucky to have me, ha! I'm just trying to uncover the facts. You must go out and win the case. That's still your plan, isn't it?"

"Yes it is. There must be at least one way to win each case and I just have to think hard enough to figure it out. Even if it's some remote legal technicality, I've got to create an argument with a winning narrative."

"Well, you sure have a winning attitude. I guess that's a good starting point."

"Thanks, Allison," I say as we get up and gather our things and start to move towards the door. "I'll walk you to the reception area. Please call me later this week after you've interviewed Maria and the neighbors."

"Will do," she says as she walks out ahead of me and I follow her down the hallway.

A hint of Allison's scent gently wafts in my direction as I walk her out. That is no ordinary perfume on no ordinary woman.

CHAPTER NINE

After a sleepless night, I walk into my office in a daze. I see the criminal complaint neatly centered on my otherwise clean desk. I think this is a bad dream and I will wake up and return to a happy or at least normal life. The Magistrate Judge's signature at the bottom reflects otherwise. This is not theory but reality. This is my new normal. I am being challenged and confronted in the most aggressive way imaginable, just as Professor Lee predicted when he questioned me in the first day of constitutional law class. I have to step up and face it head on. I have only two possible courses of action: win or quit.

I walk down the long hallway to Lou's office.

"Betty, I've got to see Lou. It's urgent."

"Well, good morning to you too, Jeff."

"I'm sorry. I am under a lot of stress with this DeMore case and I've got to see Lou."

"Lou is working on that new securities case and he has a hearing today on another matter. He's on a call and does not want to be interrupted."

"I've got to give him an update and ask for some direction on next steps. I'll go in and sit in his office until he talks to me. Even if he yells at me, I can handle it."

I open Lou's office door, enter his office and sit. I'm as quiet as a church mouse. For the longest time, he doesn't even notice while he speaks crisply into the phone. This time, he is balancing the handset between his tilted head and right shoulder. I'm surprised he doesn't have a neck ache. Finally, he grabs the handset with his right hand and slams it down. The phone could have a lawsuit for abuse.

He turns and looks at me in mild disgust and says, "What do you want?" Continuing his rant and waiving his hands in the air, he says, "I'm in the middle of two crises and I don't want to be interrupted. How'd you get in here?"

"I met with Maria DeMore and Allison Broadmore, she is the PI with Watershed Investigations. The criminal complaint prepared by the FBI against Barry DeMore is thorough and complete. They investigated for six months and estimate he stole fifty million dollars. They have flipped one of the co-conspirators and he is a cooperating witness. Allison said Barry DeMore is toast."

"Why didn't you tell me this sooner?"

"I tried. I left you messages."

"Never mind. Did you get an engagement letter and a Form 2848 Power of Attorney signed?"

"Yes, I got Ms. DeMore to sign both documents yesterday."

"Good. Get the Form 2848 mailed to the IRS so they have time to process and get us in the system as attorneys of record. Then, have what's her name at Watershed do an in-person visit and interview. Do you have any evidence to contradict Ms. DeMore's story?"

"No. I had Allison sit in on yesterday's meeting with Ms. DeMore and she doesn't see any signs of deception and does not believe the investigation will turn up anything to contradict her story."

"Be cautious, and remember the attorney-client privilege can be waived if there are outsiders present when you have confidential client discussions. I don't believe that's a problem here, but I wanted to alert you to the issue."

"Thanks. I assumed it was Okay since we are part of the same legal team representing Ms. DeMore."

"For next steps, you should review the criminal complaint to understand the facts and then begin to look for any defenses. Have Watershed complete their investigation. A good lawyer thinks from the beginning of a case about how to win. Sometimes it looks like an uphill battle, but you can figure something out."

"Sure."

"However, and there is a big however. There's a tipping point in every case and here is where any idealism you have needs to be beaten out of you. It is called Law Firm Economics 101. Did you take this subject in law school?"

"No, Sir."

"I didn't think so. Listen up," he says as he makes me uncomfortable with his serious stare. "We are here to make money, Jeff. There are many cases that are clear losers and the sooner you realize you are on the losing end, the sooner you can stop working the case and find a quick exit. You need to forget about winning for the client and focus on winning for the law firm. We do that by getting paid."

"But, Lou," I protest.

"I thought you might be too idealistic. You need to get the message. The other lawyers in the firm have commented about you to the same effect. We don't go on crusades for truth and justice here. Since we are court-appointed on this one, you should not be spending too much time. Make sure you are balancing with lots of billable time for our paying clients."

"Okay."

"Spend enough time so we don't get sued for malpractice, but nothing more. Just protect my backside. Do you understand me?"

"Yes, sir."

"By the way, I'm jammed on these other cases, and don't have a lot of extra time to help you. Short of malpractice, make yourself scarce."

I get up and scurry out. I thought I was stressed when I walked in.

CHAPTER TEN

The receptionist calls and announces, "Allison Broadmore from Watershed is holding on line one." I push the button on my office phone with the blinking light and pick the handset up.

"Hello."

"Good afternoon, Jeff, this is Allison."

"Hey Allison, how are you today?"

"I'm great. How are you faring in the midst of the storm?"

"Funny you say that. Not so well and I can explain more about that later. What's up?"

"I want to give you a quick update. I met with Maria DeMore at her home. It's really what you would expect. A small, neat and clean suburban home filled with family pictures and knick-knacks. What's remarkable is there is nothing remarkable. Her life story appears to be true. Her minivan is older and it has bald tires. There are no signs she is living beyond her means."

"Amazing. Continue."

"I also met with some of her neighbors. The picture that emerges is Barry was aloof and moody, but he was good with the kids when he was around. He was always on his cell phone, sometimes talking with his hands waiving in the air. Most weeks, he would leave on Monday morning and return on Friday evening. He told people he was swamped with the conversion over to the new fiber optic cable. The extra demands over the purchasing of massive amounts of new cable was creating a lot of pressure. He had to travel to the manufacturing companies so he could regularly check on the new cable being ordered and shipped. He was always in long meetings and client dinners and couldn't be bothered."

"Seems to follow the storyline, doesn't it?"

"Yes and the neighbors were absolutely shocked when the arrest made the news. They said he is such a regular guy. They never suspected he could be involved in something like this."

"Thanks for the update. Anything else?"

"No, that completes the neighborhood interview phase. Next, we'll search the public records to find out if Skimco owned any assets. We're moving to the financial side of the investigation."

"Thanks. Let me know because I'm really curious about what they did with the money. Fifty-four million is a lot of dough and it has to be used, spent or invested somewhere."

"Agree and we're on it."

I am in my office and thinking deeply about the facts set forth in the FBI affidavit. The complexity and effort the three co-conspirators expended in structuring and maintaining the scheme is something I never thought I'd see. Then again, I have no idea what I thought I would see. My deep thinking is interrupted when I receive a call on the interoffice phone line.

"Hello," I answer meekly.

"Jeff, it's Hillary Monroe. I'm the partner in charge of billings and collections and I'd like you to come down to my office," the voice barks.

"Sure thing," I respond, "be right there."

I walk down the hallway to Hillary's office.

I knock softly on her office door and say, "Hi Hillary, may I come in?"

"Yes, have a seat," she says firmly but without looking at me.

"I'm the partner in charge of billings and collections here at DFC and I have some questions. As you know, there is a business side to the practice of law that we need to attend to. I know you are working on the DeMore case with Lou and I'd like some information."

"Sure."

"First, have you obtained a signed engagement letter from the client?"

"Yes, the client signed yesterday."

"Good. When will you be collecting money from the client and how much do you estimate the firm will receive in cash?"

"I don't believe there will be any money collected from Ms. DeMore. I'm new here and don't know exactly how this works, but I believe the firm was court-appointed or something like that. I know a special city bar official contacted Lou and he agreed to take the case. That's about all I know."

"So, no money will be collected?"

"As far as I know, but you should discuss that with Lou. He's the supervising partner on the case."

"Okay, well Lou has been almost unreachable lately. He has been so busy the past two weeks, I thought I could get the information from you."

"Lou has been busy, that's for sure."

"Thanks for the information. Make sure you keep your personal billable hours at the high level we expect of all associates and keep your time on the DeMore case to a minimum. I want the firm to lose as little money as possible on the case. I'm sure you understand."

"Sure. Am I dismissed?"

"Yes, get back to your billable work. Quickly," she says.

I get up and scamper out. The pressure on the case mounts daily and that is just from the self-imposed forces inside the firm. Is it possible to have two opponents in a case, the IRS and your own partners?

CHAPTER ELEVEN

For two weeks, I have my head down researching the law, writing legal memoranda and assisting with document discovery. My day job as a new associate is consuming me. At the moment, I am in the file room surrounded by boxes of documents that need to be reviewed and organized. In the midst of my dreary existence, the receptionist calls and says, "Jeff, I've been trying to track you down. Allison from Watershed is on line one for you. Are you available and can I connect the call?" I say, "Yes, but let me get out of the file room and back to my office."

I run from the file room to my office and sit hurriedly in my chair. Before I can reach the phone, I pause and sneeze twice from the file room dust I just inhaled.

I pick up the phone and answer "Jeff Pearson here," I say in a stuffy, breathless voice.

"Hey Jeff, it's Allison. Long time no chat. Are you doing better?"

"We need to talk, and I'd love to tell you all about it. Maybe we can find time for lunch or dinner."

"I'd like to meet for dinner. I'm open next Thursday evening. Does that work for you?"

"Sure does. Can you find a restaurant that's convenient for you?"

"Yes, I'll make a reservation under my name at the City Grille. Is seven p.m. good?"

"Perfect. I look forward to it."

"Now that we have that taken care of, I need to give you an update on our investigation. Do you have time to talk now?"

"Yes, I would like an update."

"Our investigators combed the public records for assets owned by or registered to Skimco. We also checked with the Western Cable investigators and our law enforcement contacts."

"Sounds thorough."

"Yes, I'm always amazed at what our investigators can turn up. It's always the most interesting stuff that you wouldn't imagine they could track down. But they do."

"Did you find anything interesting in this case?"

"Just wait until I tell you. You're not going to believe your ears."

"I'll brace myself. Go ahead and hit me."

"Basically, Barry and the other two were living large and they hid it through Skimco, the Delaware LLC. Skimco collected all the profits and they would cause Skimco to buy whatever they wanted. Skimco would always take title so that nothing would be traced to them personally. While a lot of money was paid out by Skimco to the other two co-conspirators, it retained and spent a lot of cash as well."

"So, Skimco was making the money and spending it too?"

"Exactly."

"Anything more?"

"Yes, our investigators have documented that Skimco owned a private jet worth over fifteen million dollars. They even checked with the FAA and matched the tail number. Skimco also leased a Condo in Miami Beach and owned a yacht docked in a large marina nearby."

"So, the fifty-four million was used to buy assets and was distributed among them, is that what you are finding out?"

"Yes. It almost seems like they were running a business, a regular business, which they kept separate so they wouldn't get caught."

"Amazing. What happened to the assets?"

"The FBI and other federal agents have seized all of Skimco's assets on the grounds they are criminal assets used as part of the crime. The Coast Guard, with the assistance of U.S. Marshals Service, has taken the yacht to a government-run marina and the private jet is being held in a government hanger at the Fort Lauderdale, Florida airport. This is common practice in these financial fraud cases involving large sums of money. The Feds grab everything, then, after the trial is over, the stuff is auctioned off by the asset forfeiture division of U.S. Marshals Service and the proceeds taken in by the government."

"Great work. Anything else?"

"Not for now, I've got to run to a meeting. See you Thursday."

"Take care."

❖

I call Maria and ask her to meet in our offices in the same conference room so I can give her an update and get her to sign more documents. She says, other than taking the kids to school, she is free.

❖

The receptionist calls and says Maria DeMore is waiting in the conference room.

I walk into the conference room and say, "Nice to see you again, Ms. DeMore. I really enjoyed the cookies you brought last time. They were delicious."

"Glad you liked them, Mr. Pearson. They don't last long around my kids either."

"How are you doing? It's been over a month now."

"Yes, how time flies. Still no word about Barry and every day I expect him to just walk through the door. I guess my life may never be the same. One day at a time, but even that is sometimes more than I can handle. There are days I can't get out of bed in the morning. I take my kids to and from school but I find even driving around difficult."

"My thoughts and prayers are with you."

"Thank you. I'm in a fog. Make it go away."

"I read the most recent letter the IRS sent to you and it is a deficiency notice. This starts the ninety-day period that taxpayers have to either fight the case in court or give up and concede. Because there are time limits that apply, the only course of action is to file a petition with the Tax Court. Then, once the petition is filed, I will have a chance to actually sit down and talk to the lawyers for the IRS and try to get this resolved. My belief in this case is that if I can meet with the IRS and explain your situation, that it was your husband, Barry, that is alleged to have done this, not you, they will drop the case against you."

"So, something needs to be filed with a court and then you can talk to them?"

"Yes, that's what I'm saying. But in order to talk, you must protect your rights by filing a petition with the court. This is a formality to get you to the next step. Is that Okay with you?"

"Well, you're the lawyer. How would I know if it's Okay?"

"That's our only option at this point. I've prepared the petition papers and I would like you to sign them."

"Whatever you say."

"Basically, the petition says you are not liable for the deficiency asserted and, even if you are, you're an innocent spouse entitled to relief from joint and several liability on a joint return under Tax Code Section 6015 because you did not know, nor had any reason to know, of Barry's embezzlement income."

We sign the papers.

"Thanks. I will get them mailed, certified mail return receipt requested, this afternoon."

Making an effort to stay on top of swirling matters, Maria says, "Anything else we need to take care of today?"

"I understand you met with Ms. Broadmore from Watershed Investigations and had a nice visit."

"Yes, she's a nice young lady. She was sympathetic and seems to understand my terrible circumstances. I showed her around and I think she talked to some of the neighbors. Then she left."

"Then, we're done for now," I say as we both get up. "I will walk you out to the reception area," as I gently place my hand on Maria's back and follow her out the conference room door and down the hallway. She exits out the front door of the reception area.

CHAPTER TWELVE

I arrive a few minutes before seven p.m. Thursday to have dinner with Allison and I sit in the waiting area of the City Grille. Following the instructions set forth in the memo to self, I am wearing new lawyer shoes purchased with a new charge card. If a person must go into debt, shoes make a good choice I rationalize. Within minutes she arrives. I excitedly jump up to greet her.

"Allison, so great to see you again," as we share a slight, professional, embrace.

"Great to see you too, Jeff."

"Our table is ready and we can be seated."

We walk to the table and I wait for her to be seated first. Then I sit in the other chair.

"You look radiant. How are you?"

"Well, I had a hectic day at work, but it's nice to get away from it all and enjoy a quiet dinner."

"I agree. My days have become more demanding and filled with challenges. Maybe it's the moon."

We look over the menu.

Pointing at the menu, she says, "Interested in sharing an appetizer? I like the spinach dip."

"Great idea."

We order an appetizer.

"I don't want to talk too much about work, but I do want to thank you for all your help. You and your team have been invaluable," I say with a tone of gratitude.

"The DeMore case is one like no other. It's been like slowly peeling back an onion, with each layer unique. Something different each day, it seems."

"I've been dying to ask you again. How did you know about a D9 bulldozer? I'm still amazed."

"Well, as I mentioned, my Mom wanted me to be a girly girl, but I refused. I like to do things and get my hands dirty. When I was about three, I found a yellow dump truck and a shovel and I would scoop and haul for hours. When I was four, I was reported because I would not sit for circle time!"

"That's funny, but how did it affect your childhood?"

"An interesting question. That would be a long discussion. The short answer is, my Daddy wanted to run my life and I wouldn't let him. Don't get me wrong, I had a great upbringing."

"Tell me more. I enjoy your stories."

"Well, I attended the Country Day private school with eighty classmates from K through 12. Then, I was shipped off to a girl's finishing school, Mary Lawrence, in Connecticut. From an early age, I was taught to be polished and professional. I went to college with the daughters of aristocracy and captains of industry. My Daddy always had big plans for me. I summered abroad and speak three languages."

"Since you travel extensively, what is your favorite place to get away from it all?"

"That's easy. Seeley Lake in Western Montana."

"Never heard of it. Go on."

"Raised a debutante, I was supposed to get married and enter the world of high society. This was not a pipe dream like it might be for some. It was my reality. Daddy had the money, power and connections to pull it off. It was a fait accompli in his mind."

"Really?"

"What Daddy wants, Daddy gets."

"But that doesn't sound like you."

"Exactly. The idea of society lunches, art show openings and card games at the country club repulse me. I have a fierce independent streak and I'm not going to submit or give in to conventional wisdom. I want to be different and make a difference."

"I can see your independence and intelligence on display at work. You are a talented investigator with great insights into human nature. You see reality for what it is. No pretenses."

"Thanks, but it's probably more stubbornness that moves me than anything. Not always a good thing, mind you."

"So you are a rebel, is that what you're telling me?"

"A mild one. Daddy would say a wild one."

"How'd you get started as an investigator?"

"Funny story. It was the end of my junior year and I saw an ad for part-time summer help. I wanted to get away from the society gig, and working in investigations seemed about as far away as you could get. It was an adrenaline rush for me and so different from my life. I had a blast and was hooked. You get paid to peer into other people's lives and help those in some sort of crisis situation. As soon as I got out of college, I started with Watershed Investigations and have been there ever since."

"Shouldn't we order dinner? I feel if we don't stop and order, we're going to just keep talking all night."

"Agree."

She orders the fresh fish of the day and vegetables. I order the pulled pork special, without onions. My stomach, of late, cannot handle anything strong or spicy.

"What about you, Jeff. What's your story?"

"My childhood was the opposite of yours. It was filled with challenges and my home was not a happy place. My dad was a workaholic with bouts of anger and my mom basically checked out and disconnected from life. My home was a place you ran from, not to. I was alone with no one to talk to. So, my primary objective was to survive. I walked to the nearest public school. I worked from age fourteen on and have had every odd job you can imagine. I can barely speak one language."

"I'm sorry. Does not sound like a great environment for a child."

"That's true."

"How did you get interested in law school?"

"A funny story to match yours. I got a traffic ticket when I was seventeen and the policeman and judge told me to give in and admit my guilt. Since I didn't think I did anything wrong, I refused. I told them thanks, but no thanks. I would not give up or give in. I took my own case to trial and called the police officer to the witness stand on his day off. He was none too pleased."

"You did what? You stood up in court and defended yourself? What happened?"

"I won the case based on a technical reading of the traffic code. The judge said even though I was only seventeen, I should think about law school. So, I did and here I am."

"I've never heard of a kid doing that, much less actually winning. The odds were stacked against you and you beat City Hall. I can't imagine the moxie."

"Here's our food."

Our entrees are served and we eat.

"So," she says looking at me, "it seems winning and survival are ingrained in you. Is that true?"

"Well, I can't tolerate an injustice and I can't tolerate people in power taking advantage of those who aren't. Probably somehow related to me being powerless as a child and never wanting to repeat that experience again."

"I admire that about you."

"Call it a flaw, but it's not in my DNA to quit and submit."

"It's late and I need to go. Let me pay tonight and you get the next one. Deal?"

"Deal."

CHAPTER THIRTEEN

After filing the Tax Court petition, the next step is to schedule and attend a pre-trial conference with the IRS District Counsel tax lawyers representing the government. Prior to this time, I unsuccessfully tried to find someone at the IRS in a position of authority to hear Maria's story. With the facts and logic so clearly in her favor, uncontested really, I am still confident I can get the case dismissed. This is a case of mistaken identity, she didn't take the money, and once a person with settlement authority understands, I am sure the claims against Maria will be dismissed. Justice demands it. Or so I thought.

Lawyer briefcase in hand, I walk eight blocks over to the IRS' offices. My strategy is to use my charm and humor to diffuse the tension and then explain the facts and walk out victorious. If all goes according to plan, I should have good news for Maria by this afternoon.

I announce myself and am escorted into a small, cold, IRS conference room with government-issued metal furniture. There are no pictures on the wall. Three of them are waiting for me, seated on one side of the table. One of me sits alone on the other side. The man in the middle appears to be much older, late fifties, bespectacled, bald and in charge. He is wearing a dark-blue government-issued lawyer suit with telltale signs of being pressed to death. He has a discount store white permanent press shirt that is darkened and frayed along the collar. His non-descript burgundy tie is tightly knotted. The knot is much darker than the balance of the tie evidencing continued use. He might sleep in his lawyer suit and never untie the tie, for all I know. The other two are dressed as younger clones. Serious and unsmiling, their expressions remain unchanged. His soul-less eyes stare holes through me, while the other two try desperately to match his intensity.

The meeting starts poorly and ends worse as if that is even possible. The middle one speaks, while the other two government lawyers glare with furrowed brows. The glummest triplets I've ever seen. Sitting there in front of them and preparing to put my plan into action, it's like I have set the cheese and I'm about to trap myself.

"Hi, I'm Jeff Pearson, representing Maria DeMore. Nice to finally meet you."

"I'm Robert Simon, but don't call me Bob."

"Okay, Robert. My client has been living through a terrible misunderstanding and I believe that once I explain the facts to you, we can get this resolved and the case against Ms. DeMore dropped."

"How long have you been practicing law, Jeff?"

"Long enough to know my client doesn't owe any taxes."

"I was wondering, because I've never been up against a lawyer wearing braces on his teeth. I can easily mistake you for one of my interns."

"Well, you can call me a late bloomer."

"Are you trying to make fun of the federal government, Mr. Pearson?"

"No, sir, just responding to your comment."

"Well, you can stop the nonsense, Mr. Pearson."

"My client is an innocent spouse."

"Aren't they all?"

"I've interviewed my client and done an investigation and my client is innocent. She didn't take any money and doesn't owe any back taxes. I'd like to explain the facts to you."

"You can stop the pretenses and condescending tone, Mr. Pearson. I have neither the time nor the patience to listen to your antics. The IRS is the one doing the investigating and I'm going to tell you what the facts are, not the other way around. Do you understand me, son?"

"Yes, sir."

"Have you read the criminal complaint and affidavit filed by FBI Special Agent Jack Ledington and sworn to before the United States Magistrate Judge?"

"Yes."

"Good. As outlined in great detail, Barry DeMore was the ringleader of an embezzlement scheme, which involved multiple allegations of financial fraud. While I just used the word allegations these are now proven facts. Based on the amount of cash and value of assets found and seized by the federal agents, the IRS reconstructed the earnings of the criminal enterprise. Using agreed procedures, the IRS has concluded Barry DeMore stole a total of fifty-four million dollars. Since the regular tax rules apply whether you earn money or steal it, the DeMore's owe twenty million in back taxes, interest and penalties, including the special ones for fraud. Here is a pile of documents and spreadsheets that serve as the backup, so you can see exactly how we arrived at the number. The detailed calculations are all in there. Checked and crosschecked. Our agents miss nothing."

"You seized all the assets, there's nothing left?"

"Yes, it's routine in these financial fraud cases. We seize everything used in, or connected with, the criminal enterprise. There are specific federal statutes describing the crimes committed and providing for the seizure of the assets used in those crimes."

"But this involves only Mr. DeMore, not Mrs. DeMore," I say with emphasis in a manner designed to change the focus of the conversation from the guilty to the innocent.

"Interesting, but irrelevant. As married, they file joint federal Form 1040 tax returns and both are jointly and severally liable for the taxes owed by the other. All of their income is supposed to be reported on one return, their joint Form 1040 return."

"You're telling me the regular tax rules apply, even in this case?"

"That's right. The regular tax rules apply, Mr. Pearson."

"But the twenty million dollar tax figure seems too high. Mr. DeMore was not in this only himself, he had two other co-conspirators named in the criminal complaint. It seems like he is getting assigned one hundred percent of the income."

"Good observation and you are correct. Mr. DeMore is getting assigned one hundred percent of the income because he was the ringleader of the scheme. He created and ran the embezzlement and then paid kickbacks to the other two co-conspirators. Applying the regular tax rules, he gets one hundred percent of the income but no offset or deduction for the amount of the kickbacks paid to the other two."

"Why not? That's not logical. At most, he only got one-third of the money."

"Did you take an income tax class in law school, Mr. Pearson?"

"Yes, I did."

"So, applying the regular federal income tax rules, you are probably thinking DeMore has income under Tax Code Section 61, but then should get a business deduction under Section 162 for the amounts paid to the other two?"

"Yes, that would be the way the regular tax rules apply."

"Good thinking and nice try. However, you need to read further down in the statute because, while business expenses are deducted under the general rule of Section 162(a), illegal kickbacks, like the ones made here, are specifically made non-deductible under Section 162(c)(2). Illegal kickbacks that violate federal law are not deductible, Mr. Pearson. I'm sure even you would agree that would be bad public policy."

"I see your point."

"So, the twenty million dollar tax figure is the amount due for the total embezzled. Do you now have a better understanding of how we arrived at the number?"

"Yes, I do."

Continuing in a condescending tone with the intention of being unhelpful, he says, "Anything else you would like to discuss, Mr. Pearson?"

"Yes, Maria DeMore is an innocent spouse. She didn't know anything about this."

"That's really not our concern at this stage of the case. The way the regular tax rules apply, the amount of tax due is determined and then if a spouse has a defense, like innocent spouse, he or she can argue that later. There are separate procedures for that and it looks like you included her request for innocent spouse relief under Section 6015 in your petition."

"Well, I've got a lot to review," I say shaking my head. I point to the stack of documents on the table and say, "Are these all the documents?"

"Yes, these are all the documents we have for you. We have them numbered and sequenced so you can keep track of them and we can jointly refer to them at the trial you're going to lose. Also, if you refuse to agree to our version of the facts, we will file a Tax Court Rule 91(f) motion to compel stipulation of facts. Either way, we will get our way."

"Okay."

"By the way, what is your theory of the case?"

"I'm still trying to figure that out."

"You can always concede."

"Thanks, but no thanks."

I get up from the table. They stare and remain motionless. I gather the stack of documents, place them in my lawyer briefcase and prepare to leave. I quickly make my way out the door without shaking hands.

❖

After I leave the IRS' offices, I find a Men's Room. I slowly close the stall door and sit on the toilet with my head in my hands unable to move. I feel physically ill. I can't move. I start to shake.

❖

I return to my office worse for the wear. I have been sideswiped, spun around and run over by the three IRS District Counsel D9 bulldozers. Without the display of any human emotion, they showed me no mercy and gave me a legal beating of historic proportions. Walking in to the meeting I was confident and thought I could win, and rather easily, in fact. Walking out, I am devastated. They turned on me with a fury I had never experienced as an adult. I felt like a child, small and alone, being lectured to by an angry parent and sent to my room without supper. Punished for something I didn't even do, a crime I didn't commit, and in the process threatened to the core.

To them, I am the criminal and the criminal's lawyer all wrapped in one. I am the bad guy who has done all that bad stuff. Listen intently and consider my side of the story? Forget it. There is no my side of the story. Only the truth as predetermined by the IRS. I was dragged out and tied to a whipping post in ancient Rome and given fifty lashes. Just because they thought I needed it. I guess I didn't have enough experience to learn to separate my emotions from the roller coaster of events, the twists and turns. I am totally unprepared for the legal abuse being heaped upon me.

Trying to sort through my jumbled feelings is difficult enough, but there is another side to the story. What will I say to Maria? I listened carefully to her story with an appropriate degree of skepticism and even had an investigator interview her and confirm her veracity. How often do you find someone who wasn't involved in, didn't know about, and didn't benefit from, the misdeeds of others? She told her story and she is telling the truth. Now, her innocence is being rewarded with what? A bill for twenty million dollars.

It is now evident the abuse and scorn the IRS has for her husband is being jointly aimed at her. She is like the dolphin caught up in the tuna net with no means of escape. She is being held jointly liable for something she did not even jointly do. The concept of justice and rightness is being turned on its head.

Which leads my little, diminished, legal mind to ponder the ultimate end-game question. If the IRS is successful at tarring her with her husband's greasy affair, can she get her share of the confiscated money? If she is held liable, doesn't she have a claim to the loot? If she is getting the bill for dinner, why isn't she being served the meal? It seems the IRS can't have it both ways. Either she has no tax to go with her no money or she has the tax and gets the money. Will the IRS agree to that deal?

My sense of outrage is igniting and starting to burn.

I dial Allison's direct line and get her voice mail. "Allison, this is Jeff. I met with the IRS lawyers and they gave me a stack of documents. Can you meet in our offices, same conference room, tomorrow morning at nine? Call me back only if you can't make it. Otherwise, see you tomorrow."

Without time to spare, I immediately turn my attention back to the task of doing the mundane, mind numbing, document review work required of all new associates. Billable hours beckoned. Still feeling nauseous, I stop by the break room to make some green tea. There, I run into Alan Wadsworth who is an aggressive and rising star at the firm. A fourth year associate, he is on the Recruiting Committee and regarded as a leader. He can be friendly, but he is not a person I will make friends with. He leaves no doubt where I stand with him. Even if I were ahead, by chance, he will catch up and run me over. I am not his peer. Not today. Not ever.

"You don't look very good, Jeff, are you all right," says Alan as he moves slightly away from me.

"Actually, I'm not feeling so hot and need some green tea to settle my stomach."

"What's wrong got the flu?"

"No, I've been working on a number of cases at the firm and I think the stress may be getting to me."

"I know you are spending a lot of time on that DeMore pro bono case Lou brought in. Let me give you some friendly advice. If you want to make partner here at DFC, you really need to hook your star to some big clients with big cases. The kind that pays the big bucks. It's probably no secret to anyone the firm keeps a billing and collection scorecard with everyone's name on it. You are and will be ranked and compared to the other associates. The only hope you have of advancing here is to try and collect the most dollars."

"Thanks, Alan. I think I understand how the making partner game is played."

"No, you don't get it. You are too righteous. You are too concerned about doing the right thing and seeking justice. It is obvious you care more about the process and righting the wrongs of the world, instead of bringing in the cash. Stop occupying your mind with the plight of people like Maria DeMore. The system jobs folks all the time. She is not going to get you to partner. Cash is King in this place and you want to make partner and get your share, don't you?"

"Well, I guess I do want to make partner like everyone else here. It's the goal of every lawyer starting out. The brass ring."

"Exactly."

"What do you think I need to do differently? Are you telling me I need to up my game and churn out the billables?"

"Not just the billable hours, but the cash collections that go with being on the big clients. They rule, Jeff, and if you want any hope of making it, you need to angle your way in and get the plum assignments. You can't sit back and wait. Have you ever seen younger dogs in the kennel fighting over a scrap of food?"

"I hadn't thought of the metaphor until you brought it up. Maybe you are right and I need to realign my thinking," I say as I take a sip of my tea.

"That's the attitude. Start now to get on the partner track and grab what's yours."

"Thanks for the advice. I've got to get back to work."

"Will you be at the recruiting dinner this evening? Cocktails at six, dinner at seven."

"Thanks, but I don't feel up to it and I don't drink much. Maybe next time."

"How are you going to socialize with the clients and recruits if you don't drink? Anyway, you missed the last event. Make sure you don't miss any more."

I walk away clutching my mug tightly with two hands. My flame of outrage is being doused with cold water tossed by my own colleagues. If my friends are like this, what can I expect from my adversaries?

CHAPTER FOURTEEN

I am sitting in Conference Room A thumbing through the pile of IRS documents when Allison walks in.

"Hey, Allison. Good morning."

"Hey, Jeff. Your eyes are bloodshot and your hair is a mess. Normally, you look so cool and professional like nothing gets to you. Today, you look like crap. What's up?"

"You are intelligent, perceptive and like to get to the point, don't you?"

"In my line of work, I learned quickly. I can't be any other way. My job is to observe, evaluate and report. Just the facts. Force of habit."

"I thought you went to finishing school."

"I did, but that was a long time ago. Reality has beaten the niceties out me."

"Are you sure none of the finishing school charm and grace remain?"

"I guess I was finished with them before they finished me."

"You give new meaning to the term unfinished business."

"Very funny, lawyer boy."

"I had my meeting with three District Counsel lawyers representing the IRS. Before the meeting, I was confident I was going to win. After the meeting, I am now sure I am going to lose. It was the worst hour of my life."

"What happened? How could your view of the case change so dramatically?"

"I started the meeting with pleasantries and they didn't want to hear it. They pounced on me with a fury. Only one IRS lawyer did the talking, but one was enough. He made it clear from the get-go he didn't want to hear my side of story. He said the IRS had investigated and they were determining the facts. He asked me if I had read the criminal complaint and then he said those were the facts period."

"What does that mean?"

"It means since Barry DeMore is the ringleader, he is being assigned one hundred percent of the income. That means he is tagged with the full fifty-four million of income."

"And?"

"And, since the regular tax rules apply whether you steal it or earn it, all of the embezzlement income should be reported on Barry and Maria's joint Form 1040 individual tax return."

"But that doesn't make sense. He has the two co-conspirators. They got their share of the money too."

"Exactly and I pointed that out. He responded it is the IRS position Barry got all the money and then paid kickbacks to the other two. He pointed out that, while Skimco might be allowed a business deduction for the payments, there is a Section 162(c)(2) that specifically disallows a deduction for illegal kickbacks. If the payments can be characterized as illegal kickbacks under federal law, then the payments become nondeductible."

"Have you had a chance to do the research and confirm?"

"No, I plan to start the legal research after we talk today. He kept repeating all of the regular tax rules apply and that means all the income to the DeMores but the business deduction is disallowed."

"What about the assets and cash. What happened to that?"

"The lawyer said all of the assets have been confiscated by the government because they were used in the criminal enterprise. Just like you described earlier, Allison, the government has a policy of confiscating all the criminal's assets. They took the private jet, the yacht and all other assets belonging to Skimco."

"Did they turn over any documents?"

"Yes, they did and I made a copy for you. Here they are," I say as I hand a stack of documents to her. "Please take these documents and schedules and have your financial wizards look over them and see if we can poke any holes. I understand Watershed can't devote a lot of time trying to scrub the numbers. My thinking is we have no choice but to accept all the IRS numbers at face value. There's no way we can contest them. It will take too much time and energy. I can't fight a losing battle. I need to spend time trying to win the legal argument, not challenging the numbers and calculations."

"What about the innocent spouse argument. Did they listen to Maria's side of the story?"

"No, they did not want to hear it. They said that is phase two of the case. But procedurally we are at phase one and they want to take it one step at a time. To them, it goes like this. How much income and what is the amount of taxes due on that income. Applying the regular tax rules, what is the result? Then, determine the amount of the tax deficiency which they say is the twenty million dollar number."

"Anything else."

"That's about it. They did ask if I wanted to concede. As you could imagine, I said thanks but no thanks."

"Those IRS people are a gracious bunch, aren't they?"

"Yes, they will accept a full capitulation. So I guess I have that going for me, ha ha."

"What are you going to do?"

"I am feeling the weight of the IRS D9 bulldozer on my shoulders. They are trying to crush me. It's like a baseball game with a special ten run lead, game over, rule anytime after six innings. They are leading nine to nothing in the fifth inning. Basically, my back is against the wall and I have one inning left to stem the tide, fight back and change the momentum. I am losing big time and have no idea how to get out of this mess. They are treating me like I am the criminal and the criminal's lawyer. Another bad guy who needs to be whipped and stomped. They are showing no mercy and have complete confidence in their case. I'm feeling about as low as you can go."

"Have you told Maria about this latest, and possibly, last development?"

"No, I can't bear to speak to her. I can't do it."

"Well, you have given your best. You have given this case more effort than I have ever seen before. Most lawyers would have given up long ago. Obviously, this case is a loser and there's nothing you or anyone else can do to turn it around. It is what it is."

"Thanks. This is a dark day for me. One I never thought I would see, but one I must face up to."

"Your spirit is amazing. There's still a flicker in there."

"I have two requests. First, please take the documents back to your office and have your financial accounting experts look them over and see if anything is amiss. Second, it is my turn to pay for dinner. Are you available and interested? I sure hope so."

"Yes to both. That was easy! There is a new bistro that just opened and the chef is supposed to be spectacular. I will make reservations for next Wednesday at seven. Good for you?"

"You're the best." We both rise and Allison picks up her set of documents and carries them with her as we leave. "I will follow you out," I say as she leads the way out the door and down the hallway to the exit.

I see a group of four associates and four partners gather in the reception area for lunch. I ask one of the associates where they are going and he tells me the Downtown City Club. They are meeting one of the firm's large corporate clients at the wood paneled enclave. A second associate looks at me and she says, "Have you been there lately Jeff? They just remodeled and the wood and brass finishes are stunning." I say, "No, not lately. The last time I was there was a year ago when I was being recruited to the firm." They quickly turn their attention back to their group. Ignoring me, as if I am the uninvited non-member, they noisily make their way out of the reception area en mass like a gaggle of matching blue-suited geese waddling in step.

I walk out of the office and head to lunch, alone. As I walk I am so depressed I can hardly focus. My breathing is labored and my walking gait erratic. The stone cold reality is I don't have any hope in the case, I have no hope of a future in the firm and no hope in life, really. I am experiencing the trifecta of failure. This is not a pity-party this time. It is my reality. The career in law that I worked so hard to achieve and dreamed of for many years is over before it even started. I will be the first associate at Dewey, Frederick and Carlyle to not survive past my one-year anniversary. I lived life as a child, alone and hungry, and now I am a lonely, hungry adult. I have the same feelings of unmitigated despair that I had as a child. How is that possible?

How can it be that I have worked so hard yet accomplished so little? How can my life of misery be repeated? Repeatedly? Moreover, as I reflect at an even deeper level, the situation is made worse because it is the result of effort, not neglect. I have worked diligently and responsibly to move forward, yet find myself on a slow moving treadmill. With its four feet attached firmly to the ground. I worked really hard to remain stationary and achieve a new kind of failure.

I won't be making partner at DFC, so why don't I give up now and save myself the agony and effort. I won't be winning the case, so why don't I quit now. Why am I fighting any longer or any more when the outcome is painfully clear? I am a treble-hooked fish fighting on the end of the line. I will soon be netted, landed and secured. Then, carved, cooked and served up for dinner. Three experienced IRS District Counsel lawyers told me the facts and explained with precision how I am going to lose. Why don't I take their advice and walk away with my dignity intact? There is no shame in losing a hopeless case, is there?

I wait in line at the quick lunch Deli. I order a large bowl of chicken noodle soup to go and three bags of oyster crackers. I don't like Oysters but I do like their crackers. I get a bottle of cold spring water. I walk to the City Park and sit on a bench for the next hour as I ponder the meaning of life. I am a lonely loser with an embedded sense of failure and despair. I watch the squirrels bounce as they run. I finish my chicken noodle soup. Their jowls are bulging with nuts, creating the appearance of a smile as they sit and pose. They seem happy and content. They have the world by the tail. I conclude I am not a squirrel.

I do not want to go back to the office. But I cannot stay on the bench. With no other option, I have to take action, so I get up and put one foot in front of the other. I slowly, deliberately, begin to walk. My head clears slightly and I recall my most recent fortune cookie had this message waiting inside for me: "The longest journey begins with but a single step." Confucius is a wise dude. I turn his words into one step of action. Maybe, just maybe, he knows something I don't.

CHAPTER FIFTEEN

Because of the firm's billable hour requirements, I work on the DeMore case early in the morning, at lunch and in the evening hours. I do not have long periods over successive days to immerse myself in the details. I must be efficient and effective with my time. I decide to take action. Small, little, almost imperceptible, action. Laughable action to any experienced lawyer, but real to me.

I find a small, rarely used, conference room and make it my new home. Since I feel like I am being invaded and assaulted, legally speaking, I decide to call this my war room. I get the bankers file box containing the IRS documents and place it in my war room. I get pencils and pens and two yellow legal pads from the supply room and place them on the table. I buy two candy bars from the vending machine and a bottle of water. I now have a war room with war supplies.

I am in my office and receive an interoffice call from the receptionist. I answer the phone and hear a professional, teacher-like voice say, "Jeff, I received word you are using the small conference room. I know that room is never used, but firm policy provides only partners can reserve a conference room. You need to gather your stuff and leave or get a partner to reserve the room. I need the partner's signature, not just a verbal. Please take care of this immediately." I respond incredulously, "Are you serious?"

"Yes, rules are rules," she says coldly. I say "thank you" as if I am speaking to my kindergarten teacher and hang up, outraged at my elementary school treatment. When are cookies and milk served around here?

I leave my office and walk down the long hallway to Lou's office. His door is closed. I knock softly. I slowly open the door and poke my head in.

"Hi Lou. Can I ask you a question?"

"You just did," he responds gruffly without looking up.

I reflect for a moment on the rush of pain I feel when I interact with him.

"Can I ask you three questions?"

"Now you are catching on. Hurry."

"I met with the lawyers for the IRS and they believe Barry DeMore stole the money and it's all taxable income to be reported on Barry and Maria's joint tax return. They say the regular tax rules apply even if it's embezzled."

"Weren't there two other co-conspirators? What about them?"

"I pointed that out. Their position is Barry embezzled all the money and then paid kickbacks to the other two. Embezzled money is income, but kickbacks are not allowed to be deducted. There is an exception, a special rule, in Section 162(c)(2), making illegal kickbacks nondeductible."

"Never heard of that one before. Why don't you do some quick research and confirm whether the IRS is correct on the law."

"Will do. By the way, I need you to reserve the small conference room so I can use that as my war room in the case. I need a place to store documents so I won't be disturbed."

"Sure. Tell Betty I've approved and put my name down."

"Thanks."

He fully stops what he is doing and looks at me and says in a reflective tone, "Now, as bad as this case was when it first came in, it just keeps getting worse. I've never seen a case go down the tank so fast like this one. Obviously, a historic loser, so don't spend much time on this. Do enough to cover me, but don't waste a lot of billables chasing your tail. Remember what I told you about Law Firm Economics 101."

"Whatever you say."

He waives me off and says, "Now, get out of my office."

CHAPTER SIXTEEN

Applying the randomness of trial and error, I start researching the law. I am alone and have no one to ask for guidance. My objective is to see if I can poke any holes in the IRS' legal positions outlined in my pre-trial conference. My logical first stop is the firm's law library. I plan to look to see if I can find a tax book directly on point. If there is such a book, I will save a lot of time and trouble because I can open the book and peruse the index for the key topics covered, such as income tax for criminals and tax deductions for criminals. The author, a subject matter expert with decades of experience, will have done the research, described the area of law in the text and have case footnotes at the ready.

I enter the library and maneuver my way through the stacks of dusty books until I locate the tax law section. I read the gold-embossed titles on the spine of the leather-bound treatises. There is one on Corporate Taxation. One on Partnership Taxation. One on Bankruptcy Taxation. There are books applicable to specific industries, like farming and real estate, but I do not find a treatise on Criminal Taxation. Not surprisingly, I am out of luck. No such book exists. There is no explanation to be found anywhere describing this area of the tax law. Slightly frustrated, I leave the library.

I return to my office and log on to my desktop computer. My next step is to access and sign on to the legal search database on the computer. In law school, I learned to search the tax law case authorities using key words and then connectors. Case law authorities line up in order of priority with Federal District

Court decisions being the lowest and United States Supreme Court decisions being of the highest level of authority. In the rare event I find a Supreme Court tax case on point, I need look no further.

I find the tax case law database and launch a computer search using the key words that seem to capture the essence: "embezzlement and income." This search will identify all tax cases with both words in the opinion. Lo and behold, I hit the jackpot of legal research but with the worst result possible for the DeMore's. On the first spin, at the top of the list, I find the Supreme Court case of James v. United States, holding money obtained illegally through embezzlement is taxable income to the embezzler even though the law may require the embezzler to repay or return the ill gotten gains. Applying "regular" principals of income tax law, a person is taxed broadly on income "from whatever source derived." Whether you earn it or steal it, monies earned or swiped are taxed as income. This case squarely applies to my facts. The IRS lawyers are not relying on any case, but a Supreme Court case, in asserting the fifty-four million dollars of embezzled money is taxable to the embezzler, Barry DeMore. Within minutes, I have concluded the IRS is correct on the law.

Next, I research whether the DeMore's, or Skimco LLC, is entitled to a deduction for the amounts paid over to the other two co-conspirators, Scott Peters and Logan Wilborn. I read the statute, Section 162(a), which allows business taxpayers to deduct reasonable and ordinary business expenses. Compensation paid would be deductible. I then read further as the IRS lawyer suggested, and my heart falls when I find the clear and specific disallowance language of Section 162(c)(2). Any deduction otherwise allowed is made nondeductible if the payment is an illegal kickback. In this case, as set forth in the criminal complaint, Barry, Scott and Logan committed federal crimes. Payments made as kickbacks in the course of committing those crimes are not deductible. The statute is clear. If these payments can be factually characterized as kickbacks, as the IRS asserts, they win.

After thirty minutes of legal research, I find a Supreme Court case and a tax statute holding directly for the IRS and against the DeMores. I not only figure out how to lose, but confirm I will lose. The impossible is possible. Logic is out the window. The DeMore's should report the entire fifty million of embezzled funds and get no business deduction for the payments made to Peters and Wilborn. I have reached a roadblock of epic legal proportions. I have run over the spikes littered on the roadway and my tires are flat. The option to concede now looks like my only option. I wonder if Robert Simon's offer to capitulate is still on the table.

I leave my office in search of green tea. I feel sick and my stomach is churning. I run into Tim Wilson, a second-year associate, who attended the corporate client lunch at the Downtown City Club. Tim is wearing a tailored blue suit with distinctive red stripes, a starched white sea island pinpoint cotton shirt and a red silk tie. His shoes have a blinding shine that announces, "I'm in charge." I can smell the fresh shoe polish.

"Hey Tim, how are you doing?"

"Hey Jeff, I'm fine. Where've you been? I have not seen you recently. What's up?"

"Well, I've been tied up with the typical first-year associate duties and pressures."

"Too bad. You really have been missing out. The Downtown City Club is a great place to network. We met the General Counsel and staff from the Midwestern Mining Company. As you know, we do some work for them now. However, as a result of this lunch, we walked away with two new projects. The work is flowing and the DFC partners are really psyched."

"That's great news."

"To make partner, you need to attend these client business development lunches. Get your name out in the community. Be known. Build your portfolio," he says as he adjusts the gold cuff links on his French cuff shirt. I double take and look to confirm my eyes are not deceiving me. He has his initials embroidered on his cuffs, pointing outwards so I can read them.

I remove my eyes from his cuffs and look directly at him and say, "Sounds like a great opportunity and thanks for the pointer. Maybe someday I will have a portfolio to build."

"Have you been invited to lunch at the City Club? There's a group that goes almost every day."

"No, I haven't. I've had my head down and been tied up with client work and deadlines. No time for schmoozing at the moment."

"Come to think of it. I haven't seen you at any of the firm meetings or events. There was an 'all hands' meeting on the merger transaction and I don't recall you being there either. What have you been working on?"

"I've been working on the DeMore case with Lou Stevens."

"I've not heard of that matter. Are the DeMore's wealthy business owners or investors?"

"Not exactly."

"Have I heard of them? Are they part of a high tech startup?"

"No, no starting up for them," I say matter-of-factly.

"Are you working with any other associates or partners? Is there a big legal team assigned to the case?"

"No, just me and Lou. That's it," I say flatly.

"The DFC partners don't like it when lawyers have clients all to themselves. It runs counter to the firm's culture. It is important to have the perception the DeMore's are firm clients with relationships with many partners, not just one. Make sure you introduce them to as many partners as possible. The all-firm monthly client mixer is scheduled for next Thursday. Will the DeMore's be attending?"

Sensing he wants more of an explanation, I say, "No, Tim, they won't be there. Mr. DeMore travels frequently and, unfortunately, he has been missing a lot of important events during the past month. There are many people who would like to meet him, but he hasn't surfaced recently."

"Well, it seems like you're really out of the mainstream of the firm at the moment. If you are not working with a team of lawyers inside DFC and you are not out meeting clients, I'm worried about you, Jeff. But, you seem to be a personable guy, so I'm sure you will get this turned around in due time."

"Sure thing," I say as I walk away.

While I'm losing the case I'm being marginalized and alienated within the firm. This is a classic "lose-lose" proposition I never imagined being confronted with. How can this even be true? How can every single thing in my life be filled with darkness and despair? According to Tim, the second year associate, I "seem to be personable?" An obvious backhanded compliment that lingers like the sting of a slap in the face. What did I ever do to deserve these people? As I smoulder like a used campfire, I wonder why does Tim have his initials stitched on his cuff. Does he need a reminder every once in a while?

I return to my office with my cup of fresh hot green tea and the outside line on the phone rings. I slowly pick it up wondering what might be waiting for me on the other end.

"Hello, this is Jeff Pearson."

"Mr. Pearson, this is Maria DeMore. Can you talk to me now?"

"Yes, but only briefly, Ms. DeMore."

"It's been a while since we spoke and I wonder if you are making any progress on my case with the IRS?"

"The case is moving slowly and I don't really have anything to report at this time, Ms. DeMore. These matters are very complex and I need time to review the file and do the necessary legal research. When I complete these next steps, I'll give you a call."

"Okay, thanks Mr. Pearson. I know you're a busy lawyer."

"Thank you. I will call when I have something to report."

I hang up the phone and sit back in my chair and slump in resignation. I can't believe I faked my response to Maria DeMore, but I can't face her with the truth. Not yet. Not now. She will be devastated when I tell her how dire and hopeless the case is. I need to deliver the bad news at the last minute and in person. She is at least entitled to face me in person when she shows her rage. I thought I could get the matter resolved. I will end up dissolved.

CHAPTER SEVENTEEN

I arrive twenty minutes early for my Wednesday evening dinner with Allison. The Bistro is intimate, with tables packed close together. I am told to wait at the bar. I pull up a stool and the bartender asks to see my driver's license to verify I am of legal drinking age. With braces installed to straighten out my crooked teeth and correct my pathetic bite, this has become a familiar routine. She holds the license up and compares the picture to the real thing perched in front of her and, satisfied, asks what I would like to drink. I say "a sparkling water and lime" and she scoffs as if her effort to confirm I was legal was a waste of her precious time. She shoots the fizzling water in the glass, jams a sliver of lime on the rim and plunks the drink on the counter. She impatiently asks if I want anything else. I politely say "No, that's it for now." From then on she ignores me. Water drinkers must be bad tippers.

I place both hands around the glass like it is something far more precious and powerful. I stare ahead at the liquor bottles stacked by height. The mirrored glass wall is streak free and I wonder how long it takes them to so perfectly clean the glass. I feel like an imposter trying to pull off a drinking caper. I am sure others see through my non-drink drink and me. I sip and nurse it like I know what I am doing. I need to attend drinking acting school.

I am surprised then comforted when I receive a soft touch on shoulder. I am relieved to see her face. I jump up exclaiming "Allison!" and open my arms and give her a big hug. She holds me firm and slightly nuzzles her face in the soft part of my neck.

Her warmth feels glorious. Her smell is intoxicating. This is no ordinary woman.

I grab her arm like that of a long lost friend and escort her to the maître'd. With a smile, he says "right this way," and explains our quiet corner table is ready and awaiting our arrival. I follow closely behind and then move around and pull out her chair like a gentleman does for a lady. Once she is completely settled, I slide over, pull my chair out and sit down.

I reach over and put my hand on her arm and say, "It is so great to see you. I feel like you are a trusted friend I have known forever."

"I agree. We share a special connection. I can't explain it. In my line of work, this does not happen very often, I can assure you."

"That's the thing. It doesn't happen in my line of work either. I can't imagine sitting down with any of my lawyer friends and talking like we do. I feel completely at ease with you."

"I don't let people in this quickly. I have many walls to protect myself and it seems like you effortlessly hopped over them."

"Well, it's not like I planned it."

"Maybe I need to re-check my defense mechanisms and fill the moat so there are no more intruders!"

"Please keep me in the castle, fair maiden. Don't kick me out, I need you!"

"You are in, Jeffie Boy," she says, playfully touching my knee and momentarily holding it there while flicking her eyelashes.

"You are in too, Al. Can I call you Al? I can't believe I just blurted that out. Is it Okay that I said that?"

"You're amazing. That's my father's pet name for me when I was a little girl. It is a term of endearment."

"I'm relieved. The name fits you to a "T."

Why don't we stop and order. We have that talking thing between us really going. I lose track of time when I'm with you."

She orders the fresh fish with lemon butter and I order grilled chicken breast and vegetables.

"So, how are you doing in the midst of the maelstrom? You look tired and worn out. Votre joie de vivre has evaporated," she says.

"You're a perceptive, French-trained eagle-eyed PI and I am not going to try to lead you on."

"I'm really worried about your health. This level of intensity would drag down most mere mortals. The fact you are still standing, speaking and functioning is beyond me."

"Loosely translated, how would you say, 'I feel terrible today' in French?"

" Je me sens terrible aujourd'hui."

"And how about 'I shake with fear.'"

"Je trembles de peur."

"Thanks. That about sums it up."

"I can't believe you, of all people, are feeling terrible and trembling in fear. In French no less. Tell me what's going on and start at the beginning."

"I feel I am being attacked on two fronts. Inside the law firm and outside from the IRS on the DeMore case. Which would you like first? Shall I start with the latest developments on DeMore?"

"Yes, start with the case, please."

"I began my legal research with the goal of trying to find any weakness in the government's legal argument. I went to the law library and looked through the law books and there were none that apply. So, I next went online to search the tax law database in a legal search website. You type key words and then hit enter in the 'search' box. The computer program performs a key word search and every tax law case with those words will appear. To narrow your search universe and limit the number of cases, it is important to use key words that most describe the facts of your case. I typed in the words 'embezzlement and income' since that is what the IRS is saying this case is about. Do you know what pops up?"

"No, I can't even imagine with those two words."

“A 1961 Supreme Court case called James. In the case, James embezzled money from a pension fund. The IRS said taxes were due on the stolen money, but he argued it was not really his income since he had a legal duty to return the booty. How can he be taxed on income when the money is not legally his to keep?”

“That’s a great question and sounds like it is the same as what Barry DeMore did. I’m sure he has a duty to give his embezzlement money back and can’t keep it.”

“Yes, it’s the same legal theory. The argument is a person should not be taxed on money you’re legally not entitled to keep.”

“Exactly. So what happened in the case?”

“The Supreme Court reversed prior law and for the first time held embezzled funds are taxable to the embezzler. Whether you earn it or steal it, and even if you have a later duty to return it, you are taxed on it. The highest court in the land has ruled in favor of the position the IRS is taking against Barry DeMore.”

“That’s terrible news. Any wiggle room on case. Anything to distinguish it?”

“No, not that I can see. Then, after researching the cases, I went to the statute in the Tax Code. Bad news again. The statute is clear that, if the payments made by Barry to the other two co-conspirators, Scott and Logan, are characterized as illegal kickbacks, the amount of the kickbacks is not deductible.”

“Any way to argue your way out of that rule?”

“Maybe. It becomes a fact question. The key is whether the payments are factually treated as illegal kickbacks. If the IRS can convince the court the payments are, in fact, illegal kickbacks, they win the case.”

“I’m stunned. Are you telling me your legal research shows Barry and Maria DeMore must report one hundred percent of the embezzlement but get no offsetting deduction for the amounts paid over to Scott and Logan?”

“Correct.”

"That's absurd. In our investigation, we found over two-thirds of the money went to them. We have it documented and the IRS schedules even show the same result."

"So, are you saying, everybody agrees the money was split three ways?"

"Yes, clear and uncontested," she says with conviction.

"That is interesting but I guess I shouldn't be surprised. There were three of them and their deal was to split the money three ways."

"That is exactly what happened."

"Here's our dinner. I'm not too hungry but I do need to eat. Bon appetit!"

"I didn't know you spoke some French."

"I don't. With me, where I grew up, the only things French were the fries."

We eat dinner.

"I hate to give you indigestion, but I'm so curious," she says touching my hand. "What is going on with you at the law firm?"

"When you join a law firm, any lawyer worth his or her salt wants to make partner. It's the brass ring and you do everything humanly possible to reach for it. I'm sure it's the same in your line of work."

"Not as competitive, but the same idea. The partners are the owners and you want to be one."

"The partners and associates are telling me the same thing. To make partner, I need to bill a lot of hours and collect the most money possible. My supervising partner, Lou Stevens, lectured me on the importance of Law Firm Economics 101. This can be translated to mean Cash is King."

"But you are in a profession with a duty to your clients. All your clients deserve help and are entitled to justice whether they are rich or poor."

"That is the way I feel and why I went to law school. I want to use my talents and abilities to make a difference. If somebody like Maria DeMore is getting a raw deal, she deserves legal help. Her rights need to be defended and no one else at the firm has stepped up."

"I like that about you. Your vision is not clouded by money or power. You see things for what they are. Maria needs you desperately, you know that."

"That's the paradox. The more effort I devote to Maria's case, the less successful I am at the firm."

"Sounds like a great literary work. You can call it Paradox Lost."

"That's clever. But my problem is serious. I'm not meeting the big corporate clients nor working on the big deals. I am invisible. I see them laugh as they gather and go to lunch at the Downtown City Club, but I am not invited."

"I would not be consumed by worry. You are an extraordinarily talented lawyer who has a good heart. I am sure, given time, things will work the best for you at your firm."

"Thanks," as I crack a smile. I say, "Your kind words of support mean so much to me. I'll get the check this time and walk you to the door."

"Tomorrow has to be a better day."

"You are special," I say as I reach and briefly place my hand on top of her soft hand.

"That makes one of us. According to your firm, you are not!"

"One last question," I say as we get up from the table and begin to walk out of the Bistro. "What's the name of the perfume you have on?"

"Dangerous," she says in a deep tone as she looks back at me over her shoulder with mischievous eyes.

"Yes you are," I say in my confident lawyer voice.

CHAPTER EIGHTEEN

The paradox has appeared and descended on me like a dark cloud. I can see the rock to my right and the hard place to my left. I feel the stress and pain of what it is like to be between them. I feel like my life started out in darkness and after some intervening years spent wandering around in patchy sunlight, I traveled full circle and returned to the same dark spot. I worked so diligently to better myself, to escape, only to find myself in the same, intransigent, state of despair. I never wanted to experience these painful feelings again only to feel the identical, familiar, painful feelings again. I am in a territory I know all too well, except it is the territory I was running from. I ran out the front of the asylum only to sneak around the complex and reenter from the back door. I am sprinting to escape, but my feet are only powering the stationary treadmill. I am a magician going "abracadabra" except nothing happens when I move the red cape. Embarrassed, I need to give the audience a full refund, and quickly leave town.

Trying to look at things slightly differently, the paradox reappears with a vengeance. Nothing in my professional life is at it appears. Nothing is, as I want it to be. How can I be in a state of perfect cognitive dissonance? My thoughts and logic are at odds, producing illogical conclusions. My power of reason seems worthless. My ability to make sense of things is completely and utterly disconnected from reality.

I dreamed of working at a law firm. I dreamed of being a lawyer for businessmen and businesswomen who had interesting legal problems. I dreamed of working with a cohesive team of lawyer colleagues. We would act, counsel and mentor each other like family. One big happy one. I would be respected and respectful. I would start on small age-appropriate new lawyer projects and gradually work my way up the ladder. My career would advance in perfect stair steps upward towards one day making it into the partnership. I would have schmoozed with clients and built a portfolio, just as the older associates suggested. I would have done everything and be greeted with a "Great job, Pearson!" My shoes shined and shirt cuffs embroidered with my initials, I would project the positive image of legal success.

Instead of law firm success, I have experienced law firm alienation. They are brilliant blue-suited geese and I'm a boring black and white penguin marooned on a tropical legal island. I am alone and without anyone to guide me. I cannot reserve a conference room without parental partner supervision. Lou tells me I am using up his precious office oxygen and I need to hurry and get out. If I mistakenly ask if I may ask a question, I am corrected until I hit the buzzer and yell, "can I ask three questions?" Why do I need a spare? It is like everything and everybody in the firm is coin operated. If you don't have the correct change and the correct coin handy, you are out of luck and will be denied admission. Help is behind the glass, but always beyond reach and inaccessible. Use the oxygen in the hallway, not in my office, I am told.

I am not a criminal and have no plans to become one. I am not a criminal lawyer and have no plans to represent one. How did I draw the short straw and get assigned to the one case in the firm with one? I have been assigned the losing criminal tax case when I want to be assigned the winning case involving the rest of non-criminal humanity. Like a customer returning clothes that don't fit in exchange for another size, can I return this criminal project in exchange for a non-criminal one? Where is the "return/exchange" window in the firm? Do I need to get a ticket and wait patiently until my number is called?

After conducting basic legal research, I have confirmed my losing case will be lost. I thought I could win and get the case resolved easily if only I could find someone I could talk to. Like a child who could do only wrong, I am lectured by Robert "don't call me Bob" Simon and told to sit still and keep my hands, feet and all objects to myself. Only he could speak and only he could explain the facts. Then, only he would explain the law to me in such a way that Maria DeMore would be taxed on her husband's stolen money. One hundred percent, without offset or deduction for the sixty-six and two-thirds percent taken by the other two co-conspirators. She gets one-third of the income from her husband's stolen money and two-thirds of the income from two criminals she never met. How is it possible a person can owe taxes on money taken by people you don't even know?

The more I focus on this last point, the more outraged I become. I am totally consumed with the case. My childhood shame tape is playing over and over in my mind. I always lost as a child and I will always lose as an adult. I was not worthy or good enough then and I am not worthy and incompetent now. I am not only dragging myself into the mud, but I am taking Maria DeMore with me. My incompetence is directly and adversely affecting her. She does not deserve this and she does not deserve me.

This is real. It is over. This is not Officer Hernandez I am up against in City Municipal Court on some silly traffic ticket. This is the IRS as represented by the single most serious person I have met in my life. I know Robert Simon sleeps in his suits so he can be ready to pounce on unsuspecting taxpayers day or night. Weekends too. I know he has practiced and perfected his craft over thirty years just so he can get me. He didn't like my antics and told me I could be easily confused with one of his interns. How much abuse can a person take? If it's me, the answer is a whole lot. Continuously poured over me with a large soup ladle. I hope he feels better after dishing it out because I can assure you I feel worse for having been the recipient.

What do I tell Maria? I can't face her. My mind is racing forward. She and her innocent children will owe these back taxes for the rest of her life. IRS collection officers will hound her in perpetuity. Tax liens will be filed and her credit score will drop to zero. She will never get a credit card again. She will be driving the same minivan because she will not qualify for a car loan. She will be utterly and completely ruined. How do I explain the level of economic devastation that will befall her? Do I go into details or do I just let her Titanic of a tax problem steam straight ahead into the IRS iceberg just over the horizon? When she calls me in a year to ask for advice, will I tell her I am so sorry I didn't do a better job on her case? Do I mail a condolence card expressing my sincere apologies for her pain and suffering?

I cannot function. Failure is a demanding master. I am a loser losing a loser of a case. Game. Set. Match. I need to walk away and retreat to the silence of the loser's locker room.

CHAPTER NINETEEN

Distraught, I call Allison and ask if we can meet at her place. I explain I feel like I am having a nervous breakdown and need some time away to collect my thoughts. She says "sure, anything," and asks me to give her some time to get there first. She tells me not to stop, as she will bring Chinese take-out and console me. She is not surprised and has been expecting this moment for the past few weeks. I run out of my office and leave my computer terminal running and briefcase in the corner. If I quit or get fired, now the two most likely outcomes, there will be no need for them. Kind of like Army surplus after the war. Likely to be collected and sold off for pennies on the dollar. I hope the next legal occupant has better luck.

I arrive at her townhouse and lightly lift and tap the large brass doorknocker mounted prominently on the freshly painted townhouse door. After a slight delay, I can hear her feet as she runs to the door. She opens it and I lunge into her arms.

She is wearing a designer tracksuit and her long brown hair is pulled back into a tight ponytail. She looks remarkably fresh and alert for the end of the day. Her natural beauty captivates me and she is wearing a different, French, perfume with a hint of jasmine, not that I would actually know the difference and be able to pick one out of a lineup. I secretly hope that will be another matter for another day.

"So sorry to impose on you, Allison, but I need to get away. I don't know what else to do," I say as I leave her embrace and hold her hand for a moment.

"I've been expecting this. You cannot continue with the pressure you are under."

"Before this, I thought pressure was only for tires."

"You are lucky you don't have a cork. It would have popped like a cork in a shaken champagne bottle."

"I need to thank my lucky stars I'm cork-free."

"Have a seat on the couch. Would you like a sparkling water and lime?"

"Yes, please. My drink of choice," I say as I walk over and sit down.

"I have some Chinese food takeout and chopsticks. Now or later?"

"Later. My stomach is tight. I need to wind down."

I look around her townhouse and admire her furnishings and decorating details.

"Your townhouse has a warm and cozy feel. Did you decorate?"

"Yes, as a matter of fact, I did."

"It looks like your taste. Elegant, neutral tones. Soft, fluffy pillows. It smells so fresh. Like there's a hint of vanilla."

"Do you know about decorating?"

"Not even cake decorating."

"I just pictured you with a white baker's hat, ready to spring into action with icing in hand. You look like a goofball."

"Actually, there is no decorating for me at the moment. Nothing I have matches. I'm trying to transition from school mode to some entry-level of decency."

"I'm sure you will get there in time. You dress well, so you have your priorities in order."

"I cannot stop thinking about the case. My mind is consumed with worry."

"I can see why. It is a whopper."

"I've figured out the ways to lose, but I need to keep concentrating until I find the one way to win."

"I admire your focus on the goal line."

"I keep driving to avoid failure, but I've hit the biggest roadblock and my tires are flat."

"I know you don't want to admit it, but other lawyers would have quit miles ago," she says with an air of resignation.

"That thought is not going to help Maria, but I'm afraid the case is hopeless."

"Look, these are circumstances beyond your control. You didn't embezzle the money. You need to stop making it personal. It's not your taxes under fire," she says in a consoling tone.

"I know. My worry is not helping."

"Let me get the food and bring it over. You need to eat, buster."

"You know me well. My blood sugar is on the decline."

She brings the Chinese food takeout containers over to the coffee table in front of the couch and sits down with her legs folded.

We eat.

"Here is your fortune cookie," she says as she hands it to me. "Crack it open."

"Get this," I say holding the little paper with two hands. "Mine says, 'Our greatest glory is not in never falling, but in rising every time we do.' What does yours say, Allison?"

"We should feel sorrow, but not sink under its oppression."

"Wow. Those are deep. I have not paid much attention in the past. I guess I need to listen to the wisdom of a thousand years and consider the bigger meaning. Maybe Confucius is channeling his wisdom to me now."

"Let me translate for you, lawyer boy," she says as she looks directly at me and speaks in a lecturing tone. "The truth is you can't win every case and getting into the Dewey partnership is not that important. You don't need a share of profits to be a better person. Far from it."

I think for a moment as the words sink in and say, "You just used the words partnership and profits, didn't you?"

"Yes, I was referring to the law partnership. You don't need to worry about that. Missing out on some stupid partnership profits will not define you one way or another."

I ponder and say, "Partnership and profits. Humm..."

"What is it about partnership profits that catches your attention?"

"Al, I think you are on to something."

"I'm really confused," she says as she turns her head and loses any expression.

"At my meeting with the IRS, they kept telling me all the regular tax rules apply to criminals."

"Go on."

"If the regular rules apply, then all of the tax rules should apply."

"What do you mean? There are more rules to consider?"

"Exactly!"

"What other ones are there?"

"The partnership ones."

"The partnership ones? Now you are really confusing me."

"You mentioned the law firm and how they share in profits," I say.

"True, but how does that apply to criminals?"

"Al, the partners in a law firm are always talking about how they get to share in the income of the partnership. They get the profits left over, right?"

"Agree ... and?"

"Meaning that what we are dealing with is a partnership of crime."

"A what?"

"A partnership of crime. Follow me here. You told me the schedules given to us by the IRS show Barry, Scott and Logan split the embezzlement money equally, one-third each, correct?"

"Yes, our investigators and the IRS schedules show the same thing. A one-third split of the money."

"That means if Skimco LLC is a partnership, then it had three partners. And just like the partners in a law firm, they divide up the profits three ways."

"Go on."

"That means it is a partnership of crime."

"With the result that..."

"With the result that the payments to Scott and Logan, the two co-conspirators, are not kickbacks but instead are allocations of income. There are three partners total and they get one-third each."

"Allocations of income from a partnership of crime?"

"Bingo," I say in an excited tone. "Let's move over to your dining table. Get some paper and pens. I need to diagram this before I lose the thought."

I walk over to the table and Allison walks to the kitchen, opens a drawer, and finds paper and pens. Turning back, she walks to the table and sets the paper and pens down in front of me.

"I took a partnership tax class as an elective my senior year in law school. I learned the subject and I'm shocked the knowledge is applying so quickly in the real world."

"Life can be puzzling at times, that's for sure."

"A partnership is a flow through entity in which the taxable income is determined at the partnership level, but the income is then allocated to the individual partners. The partners end up reporting the income on their individual returns and paying the taxes due. The partnership, itself, doesn't pay any taxes. Follow so far?"

"I think so. Go slow."

"A partnership first computes its taxable income by adding up all the income it earns for the year and then subtracting its deductions. Then, the difference, the net income resulting, is allocated among the partners. The partners report their share of the income on their individual return. They pay the amount of taxes due each year based on their total individual income earned plus their share of the income earned by the partnership," I say.

"So, a partnership uses a two step process. First, it determines partnership income and then allocates that income to the partners?"

"Exactly."

"So, are you saying Skimco LLC had partnership income and then should allocate that income equally to the three partners?"

"Yes, that is the way it should work," I say hesitating and slightly questioning my own words.

"But Skimco LLC has 'LLC' in its name, which means it's a limited liability company, I believe. Does that matter?"

"Good catch. No, the partnership tax rules generally apply to a limited liability company."

"I'm just asking because we work with LLC's all the time. It seems that whenever we investigate a business it is organized as an LLC with the taxes flowing through."

"My professor said they are the entity of choice."

"As I think through the details of the investigation, I don't believe we found a written partnership agreement. I can go back and confirm. Does that matter?"

"No, it doesn't. The definition of a partnership for purposes of the partnership tax rules is very broad. I will confirm, but I am sure my tax professor said the partners don't need an agreement in writing. They can have an oral agreement. Even an oral agreement carried out by the parties is sufficient to make a partnership."

"Well, in this case, the schedules show the money was split three ways. So, that would be consistent with a one-third sharing of partnership income. That would be the result of their oral agreement to equally share profits."

"The facts match the theory," I say nodding my head in approval.

"What about the kickback argument by the IRS?"

I pause to reflect and say, "Well, it shouldn't apply. The three of them were in the embezzlement scheme together. They were partners together in a partnership they formed to carry out the crime. They jointly carried out the criminal venture and then shared in the profits."

"I see, so it's like they were in business together and they shared the income they made from the business. Is that the idea?"

"Yes. They were partners in a partnership of crime. Nothing more. Nothing less."

We stare at each other with our mouths open in a temporary state of disbelief.

"I'm trying to catch my breath and my heart is racing. Is this for real?

"As real as anything in this case."

"Do you think you can pull this off?"

"I don't have a choice. This is the winning narrative I've been searching for. It hangs together and matches the facts."

"The more we talk it through, the more logical it appears. Or, maybe, just less outrageous," she says with a slight smile.

"All right. So, if there is a partnership of crime, two-thirds of the fifty-four million dollars will be allocated to Scott and Logan as their share of the partnership's income. That means they get eighteen million each or a total of thirty-six million dollars. Barry is left with his share of eighteen million dollars."

"Wow," she says as she looks at me. "That's amazing to even think about."

"After your initial investigation, how did you describe Skimco LLC and how the embezzlement scheme was operated? What were the words you used?"

"I said it was like they were running a business."

"Yes, that's it. Like they were running a business," I say slowly repeating the words.

"Both our investigation and the IRS schedules show income earned and assets involved."

"That means this business has business assets and business deductions, just like a regular operating business. This is consistent because the IRS lawyers told me all the regular tax rules apply."

"That does make sense."

"As I think about it, I have a theory. The first case in my property class was Pierson v. Post, holding that if you have possession of personal property, you have legal title. Possession is nine-tenths of the law. Here, Barry and his buddies had possession of a private jet; a yacht in Florida and other assets listed on the IRS schedules. True?"

"All true."

"And you found, and the IRS lawyers confirmed, the U.S. Marshals confiscated the assets because they were owned by and used in pursuance of a criminal enterprise. Right?"

"Right."

"So, based on my first case in Property class, Barry had possession of and title to the jet and yacht. Based on their ownership and use of those assets in the criminal business, that means only one thing," I say, my voice rising in confidence.

"I'm afraid to ask what that might be," she says sitting up.

"Deductions! Write offs," I say, excitedly. "We can deduct and write-off the jet and yacht as business expenses."

"You cannot be serious."

"If I keep going, I may be able to stand up in federal court and say, your honor, we are not only not liable for these taxes, but we want a REFUND!"

"Oh my God."

"This is the breakthrough! This is it!"

"So we turn it around and treat it as a partnership of crime with allocations of income and write-offs?"

"Yes," I say excitedly. "You did it, Al, you did it. You figured it out!"

"Do you mean Maria and her children won't be stuck with these taxes for the rest of their life?"

"If I can prove the case, that is exactly what this means."

"This is so overwhelming. I am going to cry," she says as she sobs quietly and gently wipes her tears of joy.

"I need to prove the case in court and I need a witness. Do you know a good accountant?"

"Yes, I use Daddy's accountant. He's incredible and I am sure he would like to help an underdog taxpayer like this one."

"Can you call him?"

"Yes, I will first thing tomorrow. Now, let me give you a big hug, you big lug. I can't believe you!" At that moment, we jump up and leap into each other's arms like happy high schoolers.

"We did it, Al. We are gonna win this thing," I say as I hold her close.

I don't want to let her go. I don't want this moment to end.

CHAPTER TWENTY

For the first time in months, I wake up energized. I feel, happy, excited and relieved like I have been pounding on a tall concrete wall with a sledgehammer for months with nothing to show for it and then suddenly break through to the other side. At this moment, beautiful streams of light pour in through the little hole I made. Like the shining beams of sunlight, I am liberated. The dark cloud is starting to lift. Sunlight, and the hope it inspires, is taking its place. I feel alive.

I stop by my favorite coffee shop on the way to the office. I order a blended Americano and the morning newspaper. My work stress is slightly less than the last time I visited. I crack a smile and say "thank you" to the barista when my hot steaming drink is set on the counter. I sit down and place two hands around my coffee and smell the fresh ground aroma. I take it in a second time to savor the smell and commit it to pleasant memory.

I open the paper and settle in to enjoy. I start with the daily chuckle that makes me chuckle and the daily prayer: "Lord, grant me the strength to persevere." I feel a knowing acceptance of the message and sense my anxiety level slightly ratcheting down. My blood pressure seems lower and I don't have any sense of blood coursing through my veins. I turn the pages and imagine someday I will have a new mattress and matching bedroom suite, just like the one in the full-page color ad. Hope is no longer a stranger. I almost feel normal. I am wearing new black leather tie shoes and look down to admire. The new shoe leather aroma fills my senses. I feel I've earned the right to wear them. Proudly. I'm a lawyer wearing lawyer shoes doing real lawyer work. I need to harness this momentum.

I walk into my office with a new vigor. I notice the contents are just as I left them. Computer terminal running with the monitor in perpetual sleep mode. My briefcase is still in the corner on the floor undisturbed. Criminal complaint stacked neatly on top of the desk.

The last time I was here I believed it to be the end of my road. The next person in this office would be the one with a box, cleaning it out and wondering whatever happened to what's-his-name the former occupant. But like the mythical Phoenix, I've returned, rising upward from the ashes of defeat. I have one purpose. Win.

I start my legal research anew with hope for the possibilities instead of fear of the outcome. I check the partnership tax law and read the regulations. I find a section with terms defined. A "partnership" is created when two or more participants join together in a mutual undertaking to carry on a trade, business, financial operation or venture and divide the profits among them. A "partner" means a member of a partnership. A "partnership agreement" includes the original agreement and any modifications later made, agreed to by all the partners. The agreement can be oral or written. A partnership agreement may be modified in subsequent taxable years. If there is any matter not covered by the agreement, the provisions of local law are considered part of the agreement.

My phone rings.

"Hello, Jeff Pearson here."

"Hey, it's Al. I had a dream you pulled a wagon out of the muck with your bare hands. It was like a Roman movie where the strong guy does the impossible and the onlookers can't believe it. Like it was a miracle feat of strength that cannot be explained. I jumped in your arms screaming with joy."

"Sounds like the makings of a great Saturday matinee movie trailer."

"Yes, that's what it was. A short clip from a movie soon to be appearing in a theater near you."

"I can visualize the picture on the movie poster. I have one arm around you and you appear breathless. Your clothes are slightly torn in strategic places. A thrilling, epic, adventure, to be sure."

"Jeff, I woke up in a cold sweat, which never happens. Did you and I actually figure out the case last night or was that a dream too? Did I have two dreams or just one with you as the Roman hero?"

"I'm pleased to report you had only one dream. The partnership of crime is real."

"After the constant despair we've experienced in this case, I'm having a hard time grasping this new reality today. I pinch myself and it hurts."

"Have you called your accountant? I need help."

"Yes, his name is Larry Cobb and I just spoke to him. He said he would like to help out. I had a hard time explaining what this case involves, but I am sure you can fill in the details."

"I will be the first to admit I don't understand all the nuances and I need to talk it through with someone like Larry who has experience filling out tax returns and computing the taxes due."

"Larry is in his office and available. Can you meet me there at eleven a.m.?

"Yes and thanks. This does seem like a dream doesn't it?"

"I feel like I'm on a movie set where nothing is real at the moment."

"See you soon."

❖

I walk down to Lou's office. I knock softly and open his office door. His head is buried in legal papers and he is deep in thought.

"Hi Lou. Can I ask you two questions?"

"Shows you are thinking ahead. Well done, lad. Proceed."

"I have had a breakthrough in the DeMore case. I think I've figured out a way to win."

"Explain."

"Barry didn't embezzle the money and pay kickbacks to the other two co-conspirators. Instead, the three of them entered into a partnership of crime."

"A partnership of what are you talking about?"

"A partnership of crime that acted like a business, made money and has deductions and reports income out to the three partners."

"Are you serious?"

"Yes, sir."

"Did you take a partnership tax course in law school?"

"Yes, as a matter of fact, I did."

"Did you learn anything?"

I struggle mightily to contain my outrage and refrain from throwing the thick book balancing on the edge of his desk. The arrogance of this man is breathtaking and seemingly without limit or boundary.

Looking straight at him and without breaking eye contact I say, "Yes and I learned a partnership exists whenever two or more people get together in a joint undertaking and share the profits. I learned a partnership agreement could be oral. It does not have to be in writing. What matters is if two or more people get together with the intent to conduct a venture together and jointly share the profits. Just like this law firm does."

"Just checking," he says only slightly more convinced I know what I'm talking about.

"I've done the research, Lou. I'm confident I'm on to something. I have a meeting scheduled with a tax accountant at eleven a.m. to test out my theory and get his perspective and ask whether he can put the numbers together."

"To be candid, I'm really skeptical. This sounds like a flight of fancy. But check it out and let me know what you find. Just don't spend too much time chasing the rabbits through the forest. I hate wasted effort."

"I remember."

"Good. You're burning daylight. Mine. Get out."

❖

I am eager to meet a professional who does not verbally abuse me. I am sure there is one out there.

CHAPTER TWENTY ONE

Carefully pulling the large custom brass door handle, I open the sparkling, etched, glass door and walk into a large, granite floor covered reception area. There are oriental rugs covering portions of the floor, made necessary because the granite stone is polished to a mirror-smooth finish. Original artwork adorns the wood paneled walls. This looks more like an investment banking firm than an accounting firm, with the name Harrison, Cobb & Partners emblazoned in large bronze letters on the wall immediately behind the reception desk. The place has an unmistaken air of moneyed seriousness.

I announce myself to the receptionist and advise I am here to see Larry Cobb. She officially instructs me to take a seat. I am good at doing what I am told. I immediately walk over and sit and gaze around the reception area. Proving I have a firm grasp of the obvious, it appears to my legal-eagle eye that I am not just meeting anybody, but somebody. Holy moly, it looks like Mr. Cobb owns the place. Allison cannot be joking about her Daddy, judging from the friends he keeps.

Returning to focus, I get up to meet the man fast approaching.

"Hi, I'm Larry Cobb. Allison has told me so much about you."

"Hello Mr. Cobb. Thanks for your time and help," as we shake hands firmly.

"Please, call me Larry. Allison called and is running a little late. Why don't we go to the conference room and get started," he says as he places his hand gently on my back and guides me to the hallway leading to the corner conference room.

"Sounds good."

We walk to and enter the conference room.

"Jeff, I would like to introduce you to my senior manager, Miranda Long. Miranda is very experienced in partnership tax matters and I've asked her to join us."

"Nice to meet you, Miranda. I am Jeff Pearson with the Dewey, Frederick law firm."

"My pleasure."

Larry Cobb must be in his mid fifties, but looks younger than a brass nameplate on the wall would otherwise suggest. Upon close inspection, he has the obvious signs of being an accountant. Neat in appearance, perfect pencil posture, reading glasses halfway down the nose. I would hire him to do my taxes in a millisecond because of his obvious intelligence, kind demeanor and keen eye for detail. Miranda looks like the really smart girl next door who trounced everyone else in math class. I have no doubt she's as smart as a tree-full of owls. She has replaced her nerdy black kid glasses with fashionable frames, but her focused intensity says her work will be accomplished promptly and with perfection. I am in the midst of professional tax accounting excellence. No wonder I had to go to law school. I would never have survived in this environment.

Larry begins and says, "Jeff, why don't you start and give us some background on the case you are working on and how we might be able to help you."

"Will do. Maria DeMore is my client and she has a tax problem. But it's not a small one and not one of her doing."

"Sounds unusual right off the bat."

"Let me explain. Maria's husband, Barry DeMore, worked at the Western Horizon Cable Company. He and two co-conspirators, Scott Peters and Logan Wilborn, got together and, under an elaborate scheme, embezzled fifty-four million dollars from the company."

"This sounds familiar. Is this the embezzlement story that was in the papers recently?"

"Yes, this is the one. A criminal complaint was just filed against them after a six month FBI investigation. The two co-conspirators have been arrested and Barry is still missing."

"Was Maria DeMore involved? What does this have to do with her?"

"No, she wasn't involved. Barry DeMore led a double life and duped his wife and neighbors. He would leave on Monday and return on Friday, saying he was really busy with the conversion to fiber optic cable. They are shocked at the allegations. They can't believe he could be capable of thinking of something like this, let alone do it."

"Fits the movie type-cast, doesn't it? How does this involve Maria?"

"The IRS is alleging the money taken by Barry in the scheme is taxable to both Barry and Maria because they are married. The IRS reconstructed their taxable income and adjusted it way up."

"How far is up?"

"By the full fifty-four million dollar amount embezzled."

"How much in back taxes are they after?'

"If you add up taxes, interest and penalties, the total is almost twenty million."

"I've seen this before," Larry says as he sits back in his chair. "The IRS will follow the feds on these big financial fraud cases and come up with the highest number possible and throw it against the wall and see what sticks. Tax now, ask questions later."

"Exactly."

"I thought you said there were three involved in the scheme, Barry, plus two more. Why are the DeMore's getting hit with one hundred percent of the amount embezzled? There should at least be an offset or reduction for the amounts taken by the other two."

"Agree and that's a great point, Larry. The IRS acknowledges the DeMore's are being assigned one hundred percent of the income because their theory is Barry DeMore is the kingpin who embezzled the money and then paid kickbacks to the other two."

"So, the IRS is saying the fifty-four million of stolen money is taxable to Barry and then he gets no offset or deduction for the amount of the kickbacks?"

"Yes. They agree the amounts paid to the co-conspirators are generally deductible as a business expense under Section 162, but then are relying on Section 162(c)(2) for the disallowance of illegal kickbacks."

"I assume the three schemers shared the money equally, one-third each?"

"Yes, the facts are agreed and stipulated. They each got a third. There's no dispute."

"So, the DeMore's are getting taxed on the thirty-six million dollars taken by the other two, plus being taxed on Barry's own eighteen million dollar share?"

"Correct, Larry. That's the consequence of the position taken by the IRS."

"That is a typically absurd result in these types of tax cases, but the result seems plausible at first blush when you run the numbers. The simple math pencils out and the fact is all income from both spouses must be reported on their joint Form 1040 tax return. It's like a funnel with all income funneling down to their personal return."

Allison enters the conference room.

"Hi everybody, so sorry I'm late. Great to see you, Larry and Miranda."

Allison hugs Larry and then Miranda.

"Hey Allison, so good to see you again. You're almost a regular around here!"

"I agree, Larry. I helped myself to a water bottle and escorted myself to the conference room. Hope you don't mind."

"Mind? Anything for you my dear. Please, have a seat. Jeff was explaining the background. Your timing is perfect. Jeff, please continue," Larry says as he turns in my direction and we continue the conversation.

"The facts are in basic agreement. As far as the law, in my initial legal research, I found a Supreme Court case holding embezzlement income is taxable to the embezzler even if he is obligated by law to return the money. Section 162(c)(2) disallows any deduction for payments which can be characterized as illegal kickbacks under the law."

"Jeff, if your research is correct, and I have no doubt it is, then the IRS has got you. The case is an unfortunate loser for Ms. DeMore. It's a tragedy, but the tax laws are a matter of fact rather than a matter of equity to be changed later if someone doesn't like the result."

"Not so fast," I say.

"What do you mean, Jeff?"

"I have a different view of the case which, I believe, produces a winning narrative."

"Just wait until you hear this, Larry," Allison announces excitedly as she leans forward and moves to the edge of her seat.

"I'm all ears, but what could this be except as described by the IRS?"

"A partnership of crime."

"A partnership of what," Larry says as he looks at me incredulously.

"A partnership of crime," I say as he looks at me totally confused and unconvinced this is anything other than nonsense. "Let me explain," I say. "A partnership is any venture formed by two or more persons with the intent of jointly conducting venture business and sharing the profits among the partners, correct?"

"Miranda, that is the definition is it not?"

"Yes, Larry and fairly stated," confirms Miranda.

"The agreement to form and operate a partnership can be oral. It does not need to be in writing. And the partners can amend it from time to time. True?"

"Yes, Jeff. The definition and the oral partnership agreement language are found in the regulations," Miranda says.

"Thanks, Miranda. If my understanding of partnership tax is correct, and you just confirmed it is, then the three co-conspirators formed a partnership venture to jointly embezzle fifty-four million dollars and share the profits equally."

"I can see your theory, Jeff. Explain further," Larry says as he takes his glasses off and puts them on the table.

"My partnership theory fits the facts uncovered by both the IRS and by Watershed's investigation. Allison told me early on that Barry, Scott and Logan were actively involved in the embezzlement scheme and they split the money three ways. Her words were 'it was like they were in a business, with assets owned and revenue shared.'"

"True," Allison says as she nods in agreement.

"So, you are saying the facts line up perfectly with the partnership characterization?"

"Yes, they do Larry," I say with a look of confidence. "We have carefully analyzed the facts and these three gentlemen formed a partnership to carry out and carry on their illicit deeds. It is documented they had assets and shared the revenue, just like partners in a law firm, accounting firm or any other type of business with top line revenue."

"I'm really intrigued. What kind of assets did they own?"

"A fifteen million dollar private jet, a yacht and condo in Florida and cars just to name a few. They lived large."

"What happened to all their stuff?"

"The federal government, the U.S. Marshals Service, seized and confiscated all the assets. The private jet is sitting in a government hanger in Florida."

"I guess that is to be expected in these types of white collar criminal fraud cases."

"Yes, we confirmed the federal government can and will seize assets used in the crime. In fact, they can only seize private property if used in or produced by the criminal enterprise."

"So, according to your view, Jeff, the three criminals formed a partnership, generated revenue and purchased and used assets, much like any other business, correct?"

"Yes," I say.

"Where does that lead your tax analysis?"

"The IRS lawyers told me the regular tax rules apply whether you earn it or steal it. So, all the rules should apply. If they formed a partnership, then the partnership would report income, claim business expenses and calculate net taxable income which would be allocated to the partners three ways, in equal shares."

"Miranda, what do you think," Larry says looking in Miranda's direction.

"Larry, it sounds so crazy, but he's describing the way the partnership tax rules work. The only question is do the partnership tax rules apply to the facts of this case. The logic is there."

"I agree, Miranda," he says approvingly. "As I take a moment and think it through, there's no reason why there can't be a partnership of crime that reports its business activity like any other venture. Have you done some preliminary calculations, Jeff? How would the numbers work through?"

"Great question and that's where I need your help. I've done a rough calculation as follows. There is a top line gross income allocation of thirty-six million dollars to the two co-conspirators or eighteen million dollars to each of Scott and Logan, because the facts show they got their money off the top, and first. That leaves the Skimco LLC with eighteen million dollars of net income earned over the last three years. Larry and Miranda, does that make sense so far?"

"Yes, the partnership tax rules allow for special allocations of income," Miranda says.

"We see special allocations all the time on the partnerships we work with," Larry says. "Continue."

"But, we need to get the tax to zero, so we need one more thing."

"I shudder to think," Miranda says.

"Deductions! We need write-offs!"

"I was afraid you were going to say that, Jeff."

"Allison said this scheme was run like a business. If so, it has business deductions."

"Won't the IRS disallow those deductions on the grounds the assets owned were not used in a trade or business," Miranda says. "Therefore, no deduction for expenses under Section 162 and no cost recovery depreciation permitted under Section 168?"

"That is what's so interesting."

"What?"

"They may try, but I don't believe they'll succeed," I say.

"Why is that," Miranda asks as she turns her head slightly with a look of curiosity.

"For at least two reasons. First, possession of the assets at the time of arrest means Skimco LLC owned the items of personal property. I'm sure you've heard the expression 'possession is nine-tenths of the law,' and it applies here."

"Yes, I've heard that expression. Go on," Miranda says.

"Second, the government admits it seized the assets, which it can do only if they are used by the criminals charged with the crimes, in pursuance of, or as a result of, the criminal activity. That means they were, by definition, business assets of the criminal enterprise."

"So, the seized assets are business assets because they were seized?"

"Exactly! There is no question, and there should be no doubt," I say with a sense of confidence.

"Presented that way, your argument makes perfect sense," Miranda says. Deductions and cost recovery write offs for assets are permitted if they are owned by the business and used for a business, non-personal, purpose. The actions of the government prove Skimco LLC is entitled to the write-offs." She looks at Larry and says, "Do you agree, Larry?"

"I do agree, and I don't see any counter-argument," Larry says as he moves forward in his chair and places both hands on the table.

"What do you need them to do from the tax accounting side," Allison asks.

"Based on my meeting with the IRS lawyers, unless I totally concede and give up, they are not going to settle and resolve this matter. That means we need to prepare to go to court. At trial, I need a witness who has experience in partnership tax matters and can prepare a partnership return for each of the three years showing the income, deductions and write-offs."

"Our investigation showed the numbers are not in dispute. You can and should use the numbers set forth in the IRS schedules. I have all the documents in my office," Allison says. "I will get a complete copy sent to you."

"If we don't need to check the numbers and try and challenge them, that makes our job a lot easier and saves a lot of time," Miranda says.

"So, Miranda, can you help on this case. Can you take the IRS numbers as a given and put them in a partnership tax context?"

"Yes, I can," she says. Then, turns and looks at Larry and says, "Okay with you, Larry?"

"Yes, sure, Miranda, Larry says. He focuses his eyes intently on me and with conviction says, "I want us to help on this case. Maria DeMore is getting a bad rap in this deal and I want to see her name cleared, from a tax perspective at least."

"Then, you are available to testify, Miranda, and explain your work on Skimco LLC, the partnership in crime?"

"Yes, of course, Jeff. Once I do the work, I'll have no problem getting up in court and explaining it. I've testified twice before."

"This is fantastic. I can't thank you enough and Maria DeMore can't thank enough even more," I say with an uplifting tone.

"Jeff, I need to stay here with Larry and Miranda and work on some of my own matters, so why don't you go ahead and leave and I will catch up with you later," Allison says.

"Sure thing. Thanks all, and I know we will make a great team. This injustice needs to be turned back to justice," I say as I get up and walk out, leaving my new accounting buddies behind with Allison.

They pause and stare as if they are getting ready to conduct some serious accounting business. I run out quickly like I don't belong.

Tomorrow is a big day. I finally get my braces removed. My teeth have been incarcerated for eighteen months. My life is taking a definite turn for the better. Soon, I can eat hard candy, hard nuts and soft bubble gum. But in what order?

CHAPTER TWENTY TWO

I am in my little war room planning my version of legal war strategy. With Lou Stevens being such an arrogant grump, I have no one to gently mentor me. Or even not so gently mentor me. I shudder to think the treatment I would receive if I bounded into his office and asked for help on the most rudimentary of lawyer functions. I am left to my own devices. At this point, I could write a "do it yourself" book, not on a specific task or project, but about handling all of life. I am a generalist "do it your selfer." I don't know any other way.

I think back to my trial advocacy class and the lessons learned. Two of the most significant are be organized and be prepared. A good lawyer will never ask a question she does not know the answer to. I also think back to my first trial in municipal court. I identified my theory, proved my theory though direct examination of the witness and summarized with the law in hand.

I need to stop the internal whining machine that seems to get in the way of progress. If I went to trial as a kid, I can surely go to trial as a lawyer-adult. I am sure I know more than I give myself credit for. While hope may not be a strategy, it is my plan at the moment. I repeat the daily prayer: "Lord, grant me the strength to persevere." Given my current circumstances, it is a keeper.

I pull out my yellow legal pad and pen and start a list of action items necessary for trial. I label this my "DeMore Trial Checklist." I want to, and need to, appear prepared. I need to look like I mean business and look organized. I need to make sure Maria DeMore has confidence when she sees me standing up in court. I need to envision and pre-plan the order in which the events will unfold and then create lists which follow, or fill in, the chronology. Make a list of witnesses I want to call and exhibits I will enter into the record and use with that witness. Consider not only my direct examination of my witnesses, but consider the witnesses to be called by the government and how I intend to cross-examine them. I catch myself, realizing this is the stuff of real lawyering. Writing it down is helpful, therapeutic and necessary to perform the task at hand.

I find and label two large three ring binders. One for everything pre-trial and one I will use at the trial. The trial notebook will be critical, because, as my battle buddy, I will actually use it and follow the contents precisely as the trial unfolds. I prepare the following index tabs: Opening Statement; Stipulations of Fact; Witnesses; Exhibits; Law Citations, which will have subheadings for my table of authorities, case law research and cites to the tax law, Internal Revenue Code and regulations; Opposition Case Research; and my Closing Argument.

I walk into Lou's office with a news report rather than questions. After being verbally whipped, without mercy, I decide to implement a new strategy. A good offense should beat a good defense.

"Lou, I would like to give you a report on the DeMore case."

"I like reports of progress better than your incessant dribble of silly questions. Proceed."

"I met with two tax accountants at the accounting firm of Harrison, Cobb & Partners. I explained the facts of the case and my theory this was a partnership of crime. At first, they believed the IRS had the winning argument and there was no hope for Maria, but after I explained the partnership concept they liked it. They confirmed a partnership can be formed with an oral agreement, the agreement can be modified, and it is a joint undertaking with the objective of jointly sharing the profits."

"They agreed with your off the wall idea?"

"They did and they don't think it is so off the wall."

"They don't?"

"No. In fact, Miranda Long, a senior manager and specialist in preparing partnership tax returns, has agreed to testify."

"I am shocked they agreed to help. Typically, professionals run for the hills when they hear the troubles Maria has and the size of the mountain that needs to be climbed. It takes commitment to win, and usually other professionals only have the commitment to run. Away."

"I have the full backing of one of the name partners, Larry Cobb."

"I've heard of him. He's well respected. How on earth did you find him, much less get him to agree?"

"I was introduced by the PI I'm using, Allison at Watershed. Once Larry heard Maria's story and listened to my theory, he was willing to climb on board. I have a team consisting of Watershed Investigations and Harrison, Cobb, ready to go."

"You will need everything and more to even have a prayer. I'm stunned you have such quality folks on your team. Anything else?"

"Yes, I started preparing my three ring binder trial notebook. Would you like to look at it?"

"No, that is first year lawyer stuff and I have neither the interest nor time."

"Okay, just checking."

"Speaking of time, you're now wasting mine. Get out," he says waiving his hand.

I get out with slightly less urgency than all the times before.

I call Maria DeMore and ask her to meet me in my office tomorrow at 1 p.m. She protests slightly, explaining she has not heard from me in weeks and was beginning to wonder what was going on. She is relieved I am still on the case and can meet to provide a status update. I assure her everything has been proceeding smoothly.

With my new ability to assuage the natural, all-too-justified, fears of clients, I may consider running for political office one day.

CHAPTER TWENTY THREE

Allison has commitments with her other investigation clients, so I am waiting to meet Maria alone in Conference Room A. I position a large water bottle but only a small tissue box, hoping the passage of time has taken the sharp edge of pain away.

I am not nearly as apprehensive for this meeting as I was with the prior ones. Maybe it is a combination of experience and my newfound sense of confidence over my partnership of crime theory that allows me to temper my emotions. I still feel a lump in my throat and ill-at ease, but I am calm enough to believe I can function. Little markers of progress along my legal roadway. Maria deserves better than my previous miserable performances as her lawyer and I am trying to up my game.

Maria walks gracefully into the conference room and, after placing a tin foil covered paper place on the table, shakes my hand differently, with her two hands approvingly wrapped around mine, as if she is relieved to see an old friend. Smaller and slighter than I remember, she is shaking slightly, but seems to be worlds removed from the fragile state she displayed in our prior meetings. Her eyes are not nearly so frantic, her tears hiding in retreat. She is wearing different church clothes but her hair appears unchanged, stationed firmly in its same place. For the first time, I notice the scent of a mild perfume, which seems to clash with other smells competing for attention, such as her hair spray and her overly pressed, musty dress. It may have been stored in mothballs in a closet for some period of time. Fresh air would do the dress and Maria some good, I am sure.

She has new reading glasses and a softer shade of lipstick. She looks more normal and has a sense of resigned calm. Not all problems solved, but some put on the shelf for the time being. I conclude we both seem to be handling things better at the moment.

"Nice to see you again, Ms. DeMore."

"Please call me Maria. May I call you Jeff?"

"Yes, of course."

We sit down on opposite sides of the conference room table.

"I brought you another batch of my cinnamon nutmeg chocolate chip cookies. I figured the last batch is gone by now," she says as she slides the covered plate towards me.

"Thanks, Maria. Your cookies did not last long around here. You must have a secret recipe that causes them to disappear."

"They disappear with my kids that's for sure."

"How are you doing? Any news about Barry, have you heard anything?"

"No news. The police are looking for him and now are treating it as foul play. I still imagine he will just walk through the door and act like nothing happened. He will ask about the next Cub Scout project and what time is soccer this Saturday. I still believe he will just pop back, just as quickly as he left, he will be back," her voice trailing off as she looks away and down towards the floor.

"You look so much better. My thoughts and prayers continue to be with you and your family."

"Thanks, Jeff. How is the IRS doing? Are they going away? Can I have my life back?"

"No, they are not going away. They believe Barry embezzled a lot of money from Western Cable and they believe taxes are due."

"See my purse," she says as she opens to show the contents, "I don't have the money."

Looking inside, I say, "I know you don't."

Applying reasoned logic she says, "This is what I don't understand. If I had the money, I could pay taxes. But I don't have the money." Opening her purse wider she says, "Do you see any money in there?"

"No, I don't see any money," I say appreciating her common sense. "Your lifestyle has not changed any the past few months, has it? I have to ask the question to see if there is anything I should know about."

"Yes, as a matter of fact, my life has changed. It's gotten a lot worse. My husband is gone," she says as she sobs slightly and grabs a tissue with the tips of her fingers. She continues with an air of sadness and desperation, and says, "I have no money. The neighbors bring me food. I'm living hand-to-mouth."

"I'm so sorry."

"The not knowing is the worst part. If he's dead, I can start to grieve and move on with my life. But I don't know what to do. I don't have any answers and it's horrible. I can't claim on any of his life insurance policies and have no source of income."

"I understand."

"I don't think you could even begin," she says as her eyes narrow and focus straight ahead, her anger instantly visible and ready to boil over.

"May I give you an update on the case?"

"I assume you're not going to tell me they folded up their tent and are leaving me alone. Go ahead."

"No, they haven't budged. I'm now preparing to go to trial. Although the timing is a little fuzzy, I expect the trial to be set month after next."

"So, the trial should begin in about two months?"

"Yes, I'll keep you advised when the date is set."

"What do you plan to say at trial? Can you tell them to stop because I don't have the money?"

"At trial, I need to convince the Tax Court judge you are not liable for any of the taxes."

"How will you do that?"

"I've been working with Allison, the PI at Watershed Investigations, on developing a theory to win the case."

"You're going to try to hit this thing head-on and win the case?"

"Yes, I want to win the case and get the income reduced to zero. If you have zero income from the embezzlement scheme, you have no taxes, interest or penalties."

"No income, no taxes," she says in disbelief. "What's your theory that can possibly allow you to win the whole thing?"

"Let me explain it to you. The IRS says Barry embezzled fifty-four million dollars and then paid illegal kickbacks to the other two co-conspirators, Scott and Logan. Our investigation revealed the scheme was run like a business with an entity, Skimco LLC, collecting revenue and buying assets. The entity had three partners, Barry, Scott and Logan, who shared everything one-third each. If they jointly carried on the scheme and shared the profits equally, that means it was a partnership of crime."

"A what did you call it?"

"A partnership of crime," I say with confidence.

"What does that mean. What's the significance?"

"It means the three of them were partners in one partnership. They joined together to put the scheme in place and share the proceeds of their efforts equally."

"Can they do that?"

"They can and did do that. This scheme was run like a business. Just like this law firm has partners that operate a business and share in profits, that is exactly what they did."

"So, the income goes away?"

"Well, two thirds goes to Scott and Logan. One-third stays with Barry," I say.

"That still leaves a lot money and a lot of taxes. The numbers are huge."

"True. Barry is left with his eighteen million dollar share and something needs to be done to get that number to zero."

"What will do that?"

"Deductions! Write-offs," I say with my voice rising.

"You're talking in circles, young man."

"Like any business, this scheme has tax deductions for business expenses. It owned a private jet that can be claimed as a write off. The entity owned a lot of assets, paid rent and had many deductions, just like any business partnership."

"I'm getting faint," she says as she uses her right hand to fan her face. "Can we stop for a moment while I stand up and catch my breath."

She stands up and walks around. She returns to her seat.

"There's more good news. I explained my theory to a tax accountant and she believes in your case and is willing to help with the numbers and calculations and will testify at the trial. I need a witness and Miranda Long, a senior manager with the Harrison, Cobb & Partners accounting firm, has agreed to go to court and explain the partnership of crime to the judge."

"There's somebody else who believes this tall tale besides you?"

"Yes, there is," I say looking her straight in the eyes.

"She will get up and testify and be a witness to help me?"

"Yes."

"I'm going to cry," she says as she bursts out in uncontrollable tears.

She continues to cry.

"I'm so sorry I'm so emotional, Jeff. But this is the first bit of good news I've had since this nightmare began. You have not explained anything to me until now. I'm so overwhelmed."

She sniffles.

"I couldn't tell you what I didn't know. I just figured this out. It took me awhile to put the pieces of the puzzle together. But the facts fit the theory. The scheme looks like a partnership and if it is the numbers should work out."

"I had no hope until now," she says looking at me with tears welling up in her eyes.

"Of course, there's no guarantee the Tax Court Judge will agree, but the narrative and logic is there."

"Can you get up in court and really say this?"

"Yes, this is my theory of the case and I plan to ask Miranda to testify. She just agreed to do this. It has taken me a long time, but I think this holds water."

"No one else would take my case except you, Jeff. I had no hope. Then, when I didn't hear from you I was convinced I had no hope and I would lose and be destitute. I thought the only outcome was I would have taxes forever. Now, at least there is a chance. Is that what you are telling me, Jeff. I have a chance?"

"Yes, Maria, you have a chance. It may be slim, but it is a chance. I can't predict what will happen, of course, or even whether a judge will buy it. But it is an argument, a legal theory, that I can and will get up in court and argue."

"I'm just speechless and in shock. I can't talk anymore. I can't breath."

"I totally understand. Let's stop now and pick up in another few weeks. Then, I will have more information about the trial date and I can explain the case I plan to put on. I started my trial notebook and I'm getting ready."

"Thank you, Jeff. And thanks to Allison and those others who are helping. They are such nice people to want to help a person like me in such a mess."

"I will tell them."

"I must go."

"Let me see you out."

I carefully grab the foil covered cookie plate with my left hand and assist Maria with my right as we walk out.

I walk into my war room with cookies in tow. I am not sharing this precious cargo with any of the heathens in the office. I pull one out from its tin foil sheath and savor the cinnamon nutmeg blended aroma. I hold it close to my nose and inhale. I have never paused during business hours to smell a cookie. I am in cookie heaven. I take a small bite and my brain begins to light up with the awakening arousal of primal food instincts. These are not just cookies. This is war food belonging in my war room. I must transport, store and secure immediately. As if following orders, I close the aluminum foil tightly around the edges. I hide them, planning to tell no one of their top-secret location.

CHAPTER TWENTY FOUR

The Clerk of the Tax Court calls and confirms the trial will be held on Tuesday, December 1, at nine a.m. in the main court room at the old, ornate, former United States Post Office building. Recently renovated and converted for use by other federal courts, such as the Tax Court, the venue adds to the suspense and drama because of its high ceilings, large polished marble columns and frescoes in the ceiling. The only building downtown with gold leaf made of real gold.

I speak with Maria over the phone and advise of the court date and tell her the trial should take two full days, Tuesday and Wednesday. She asks if I am still planning to argue the crime is a partnership and I say yes, that is still my plan. She has to hang up because her cookies are burning and her children are bickering over the soccer ball. Sounds like a return to normal to me.

My war room looks like a war zone with papers flying everywhere. The first rule of trial preparation is to be organized and I am breaking the rule. I have taken the big pile and reorganized to create five smaller piles. I am frustrated because it was a lot easier to prepare for a "mock" trial in law school. There is no mocking the real trial just over the horizon.

In a slight state of panic, I dial Allison and Miranda and leave voicemail messages asking them to meet me at the firm. I need help turning this document confusion into order in the court. Also, I need to review the final partnership tax schedules Miranda and her team are preparing. I am counting on Miranda to turn my legal theory into tax return reality and am anxious about how and whether this will turn out. I feel like I'm in eighth grade science class and about to dip the litmus paper into the solution. Will I feel a relieved sense of excitement as my litmus paper changes color? For Maria's sake, I sure hope so.

❖

I walk into the conference room and Allison and Miranda are talking and comparing notes.

"Thanks for meeting me here at my office, Allison and Miranda. I'm feeling panicked as I try to organize the case for trial. I need your help, desperately."

They nod in calm understanding. They are handling this far better than crazy me.

"Miranda, let's start with you, what have you got so far?"

"Allison delivered all of the documents produced by the IRS and, per your instructions, we are taking the numbers at face value. We have simply accepted them as true and lifted them from the statements and schedules. That has saved a lot of time, because it would be time consuming to dig up the source data on a fifty-four million dollar embezzlement scheme. We could do it if we had to, but I'm being clear about what we have and have not done."

"Yes, Miranda, I don't want to challenge the numbers. I want to accept them as true. In addition to saving our pre-trial time, it will save time at trial and add an element of surprise because I am not contesting any of the substance of the government's case."

"I understand and we've followed your directions."

"Can you explain what a partnership tax return would look like for Skimco LLC during the past three years when the money was embezzled?"

"Yes, I have it here," she says as she hands out copies for Allison and me. After we get the schedule and look at it for a moment, she says, "For each year, there is a top line gross income special allocation to Scott and Logan of six million dollars. This adds up to a total of eighteen million dollars each for the three years."

"That is supported by Watershed's initial investigation. Scott and Logan got their thirty-six million dollar share off the top before any costs or expenses," I say.

"Understood. We agree and made the initial step one partnership income allocation to conform."

"Good. Proceed."

Miranda continues with the explanation of her schedule and says, "For step two, we calculated the net taxable income of the partnership. The formula is the remaining income minus the costs, expenses and tax deductions allowed for the partnership of crime. For each of the three years, the partnership had six million of income minus the costs and expenses we could document from the IRS numbers and taking depreciation and the costs of operation on the fifteen million dollar private jet."

"Jeff," Allison interjects and says, "we did some additional digging and, using the tail number of the jet, we searched the public records database available with the FAA and retraced the flights made. Once we knew the routes traveled, we calculated the cost of two pilots, fuel, landing fees and maintenance. It's all identified and determined. We also found a copy of the lease agreement on the Florida condo and deducted the monthly rental payments."

"That all sounds good, but what does it mean?

"It means that, after we reconstructed the allowable deductions and depreciation expense of the jet, your partnership of crime has a net loss for each year," Miranda says with calm efficiency.

"A what did you say?"

"A loss. The partnership operated at a tax loss.

"Let me see those, Miranda," I say as Miranda gathers another set of papers.

"Sure, here are the schedules I prepared. One for each of the three years," Miranda says as she slides the schedules on the table towards me.

I glance at the schedules and read the details. I need to probe further to make sure this can withstand challenge.

I look at Miranda and say, "Are you comfortable you have recreated the books and records of the partnership of crime and prepared the revised tax calculations in accordance with the general partnership tax rules applying to all partnerships?"

"Yes, just like a regular partnership," Miranda says confidently nodding her head.

"Are you prepared to testify at trial," looking directly at her eyes to see how she responds and what her body language conveys.

"Yes, Jeff. I'll have no problem doing so. There's nothing unusual or tricky about this. About as straightforward as you can get. No games, no gimmicks. This is basic partnership tax, the kind I do almost every day," she says calmly and with complete matter-of-fact confidence.

"Unbelievable. But this makes total sense to me. If the regular tax rules apply, they all should apply. With the amount of assets owned and expenses, this is the logical, common sense, result," I say.

I pause and take a moment to reflect. I sit back in my chair and stare out the window in a state of deep thought. Then I quickly return to reality.

"Am I missing anything here, Miranda?"

"No. Not a thing," she says without hesitation.

The three of us stop and stare at each other, stunned as if we've been hit by a meteor. No one can talk as we recognize the break-through significance of the moment.

"I want to hug you, Miranda, but I think my ethical lawyer rules don't allow for pre-trial hugging of the witnesses. I will see you at trial on December 1 and I will give you a big hug afterwards."

"Thanks, Jeff. I'm not aware of any accounting hug rules to match your lawyer ones, so I am fine either way," she says in a manner evidencing complete control.

"Please prepare your final documents and schedules so they can be introduced as exhibits at trial."

"Will do. I will arrive early on December 1 and be ready," Miranda says. Her tone and demeanor leave no doubt she will be prepared and ready for trial.

"You're the best," I say smiling and looking at Miranda, then Allison. "What a great team. Now if we can just cross the finish line!"

I am gaining strength. This is the first time in the case I've had such a feeling. With this, I know I can win.

I walk into Lou's office with my new air of confidence and authority, expecting the gruff abruptness sure to come my way. I'm a calloused abusee, better prepared for the onslaught.

"Lou, the Tax Court set Tuesday, December 1, as the trial date in the DeMore case. Shall I talk to your secretary Betty and get it on your calendar?"

"No need, Jeff. I have another trial scheduled for that week in a big securities case and I am booked. Remember Law Firm Economics 101? Well, I'm living it and will be unavailable."

"Well, what should I do, Lou? There's no one else in the firm who knows this case and no other lawyers with availability."

"The first thing you better do is show up and try the thing. If you do, I have more good news. Maria has no experience with courts so she won't even know the difference between a good lawyer and a crappy one. Surely you know enough to try a simple tax case, don't you?"

"I did take trial advocacy in law school."

"Perfect! That should be enough for you to get started. As I think about it, I've never seen a lawyer commit malpractice once they get to the courtroom."

"Any advice for me, Lou?"

Pause, as he looks to the ceiling in a moment of deep, contemplative reflection.

"Yes. Don't lose," he says with seriousness and looking directly at me.

"Thanks, Lou. That's very helpful."

"Sure thing, kid. Now, get out and be on your way. I like you best when you are scarce."

During the brief time I have been a lawyer, I have encountered mixed signals and mixed metaphors. I now discover someone who is mixed up. I can scarcely understand him.

❖

With a familiar gurgle and perpetual tightness in my stomach, I walk to the break room to get some green tea. I run into the arrogant Lou-in-training associate, Alan Wadsworth, talking with Jim Raines, the firm's managing partner. I should not be surprised at Alan's public display of sucking up to the managing partner, but there are some things beyond the pall. Why can't he suck up to the managing partner in private? Why does he need to do it in public, knowing his show is on display for all to witness. Maybe that is part of his charming, suck up, self. Maybe this is the reason, added to the litany of others, I won't be making partner. Maybe Alan is teaching me a lesson I don't want to learn.

"Hi Jim, hi Alan, sorry to interrupt," I say.

"Hello Jeff. By the way, I prefer being called James."

"Of course you do, James."

James is about fifty, with an expanding chin slightly doubled and a rounded middle, evidence of frequent lunching. Slightly balding with brown speckled glasses, he is always talking about money and clients. I guess that is why he is the managing partner, but I wonder about cause and affect. Is he the managing partner because he was always focused on money, or was he more balanced and became concerned about money only after becoming the managing partner? Whatever the cause, he is a singular money-focused machine and, without a money connection, I have nothing to discuss with him. I have no illusions I even register a blip on his law firm money making Richter scale.

"Hey Jeff, I was just giving James an update on my business networking efforts. I'm really getting traction in the corporate marketplace and the results are starting to show. I've connected with the General Counsel at Capital Industries and my relationship building is paying dividends. Yesterday, I got a call from her about another new matter. It's a small one, but little ones today add up to big ones tomorrow."

"Good for you, Alan," I say half-heartedly as I turn away and fiddle with the hot water spigot on the outside of the industrial coffee machine.

James turns in my direction and says, "How are you doing? I've not seen you around at the firm mixers and recruiting functions. What have you been working on?"

I look back at him and say, "I have my regular associate responsibilities and also have been working on my trial preparation for the DeMore case."

"Isn't that the pro bono case Lou agreed to take from the City Bar?"

"Yes, that's the one."

"It seems like the bar puts us on a list and we have to take one a year to stay in good graces. Are you collecting anything or is it just another black hole for us?"

"There are no collections. The case is set to go to trial on December 1. Maria DeMore, the client, really needs our help. Otherwise, she may owe a lot of taxes for the rest of her life. It is really serious for her and no one else will help her."

"Whatever. Do what you can to keep your time to minimum. I guess the good news is, with the trial soon, the black hole will be filling up. We don't have any excess capacity or resources available, so show up, lose, and let's be on our way. I didn't know Maria DeMore before you mentioned her case and I won't know her after. So, show up, lose quickly and let's move on."

"That's the same directive Lou delivered. Message received."

James nods my way in mocking "I don't care" approval, and ignores me as if I'm contagious, quickly turning his attention back to Alan.

"Alan, why don't you follow me back to my office," he says as he places his hand on Alan's perfectly starched white shirt and guides him away from me. As they begin to walk he says with an encouraging tone far different than the one used with me, "I'd like more details on your contacts at Capital Industries. I want to provide an update to the partners at the next partnership meeting and highlight your efforts with the General Counsel."

As Alan turns to leave with his new best friend, he looks back at me over his shoulder and cracks a wide smile with the smugness of a cat that just swallowed the bird. Life is really good for one of us. I half-smile back, hoping he chokes on the feathers. My derisive thinking further evidence of my human frailty.

CHAPTER TWENTY FIVE

I arrive at the Old Post Office building and walk down the hallway to the main courtroom. I'm thirty minutes early. I enter the courtroom through large wood doors and make my way to the taxpayer's counsel table. I take my battle buddy trial notebook out of my large briefcase and place it gently on the table as if it is precious cargo. I place two pens next to my notebook. I am ready to go. I practiced my opening statement and have my list of witnesses and the order I want to present the case. I feel confident and nervous like I did when I appeared in Municipal Court. That was kid stuff, though, and this is for real. Twenty million dollars of real serious. I store my large briefcase under the table and sit for a moment to take it all in. Not for comfort, but to control my panic. Shaking is less visible when I sit.

Maria DeMore arrives and, for the first time, I give her a spontaneous hug. The contact is awkward for us both, like hugging your cousin. Allison, Miranda and Larry Cobb arrive soon thereafter wearing what look to be matching blue suit courtroom attire and settle in on the first bench near me in the front row of the gallery. They look official and serious like they are ready to bring our case theories into the courtroom. Allison and Miranda each have a nervous appearance because they know they will be on stage soon. I feel comforted by their presence and excited to finally get on with it.

With time still to go before the case is called, I look over at Robert Simon and his team representing the IRS. I swear he is wearing the exact same government lawyer suit and soiled red tie. His shoes are old, worn and scuffed like he doesn't care. I am convinced he knows exactly what he is doing and his appearance is consistent with his attitude. He does not care one bit and this is not a good sign for me. Like Barry, I may end up toast.

As if acting on my suspicions, Robert walks over near me and asks about my theory of the case. As I begin to respond, he folds his arms in defiance and stares in disgust. I give him the same answer. "I'm still trying to figure it out," I say looking directly at him. He stares at me with his soul-less eyes and says, "You're running out of time for your antics and it is too late now with court starting in a few minutes to challenge the IRS numbers." I advise I have no plans to challenge the IRS numbers and he looks at me quizzically, in disbelief. He responds, coldly and says, "In my thirty years, every taxpayer challenges the IRS numbers proposed, that is what going to Tax Court is about." I say, "Not necessarily," and look him straight in the eyes without blinking or losing eye contact. Responding with a false sense of dismay, he says, "The truth is, you have the burden of proof and all I need to do to win is show up." He looks supremely confident, like he knows this case is in the bag.

Our sidebar conversation is interrupted when court is called into session. His last words are ones I should expect: "Good luck, kid, you're going to need all of it after I trounce you." I can only mumble and smile at his obvious gamesmanship. Under my breath, I repeat the words "stay calm and stay focused." My mantra is working. If I can just remember to periodically breathe.

"All rise. Tax Court in session. The Honorable Louise Woodruff presiding."

The judge looks regal as she strides in and takes her seat on the large high-backed leather chair located center stage. She is in her late forties and looks younger than her years, wearing fashionable reading glasses over her kind eyes. She has a reputation for being fair and taking an even-handed approach. But she does not tolerate fools lightly and expects counsel to be prepared and proceed in an orderly fashion. She is patient when speaking with taxpayers, but a little less patient when speaking with taxpayer's counsel. She likes order in the court and does not like bickering or courtroom antics. She does not favor or take extreme positions. If this were a football game, Judge Woodruff would have us playing in the middle of the field, between the forty-yard lines.

"The first case on the docket is DeMore v. Commissioner. Would counsel please announce and introduce themselves," she says into the microphone with the authority and clarity of a judges voice.

"Jeff Pearson for the taxpayer, Mrs. DeMore."

"Will Mr. DeMore be appearing, counsel?"

"No, I don't believe so at this time, Your Honor."

"Robert Simon, Ernie Sills and Brandon Magee, for the Commissioner of Internal Revenue, Your Honor."

"Three for the government and only one for the taxpayer? Who will be lead counsel?"

"Me, Robert Simon, I will lead for the government, Your Honor," as he turns and looks at me, the crushee, with utter disdain.

"I have your joint stipulation of facts which seems to be rather brief, but I will take it. Mr. Pearson, since the taxpayer has the burden of proof, I will ask you to make your opening statement first. Proceed."

I walk slowly, calmly, over to the lectern that is positioned in the middle of the courtroom between the two counsel tables. I open my trial notebook to the tab marked opening statement. I pull it out and prepare to follow the script closely. I am speaking to a judge and making a transcribed record, where every word is typed on paper at the end of the trial. I am not trying to convince or wow a jury with my impassioned eloquence. This is not ice-skating and there are no extra points for style. What matters are the words spoken, not the way they are spoken.

"Your Honor, may it please the court. My name is Jeff Pearson and I am here representing the taxpayer, Maria DeMore. Mrs. DeMore is seated to my right at counsel's table."

"Welcome, Mrs. DeMore," the judge acknowledges with a kind tone as she looks directly at Maria.

"This is a case of mistaken identity. Maria DeMore did not do anything wrong and does not owe any taxes.

First, some background. Her husband, Barry DeMore, is accused of taking a lot of money from his company that did not belong to him. He and two co-conspirators, Scott Peters and Logan Wilborn, are accused of embezzling fifty-four million dollars over a three-year period in a jointly run scheme. The facts are clear there were only three involved and they shared the ill-gotten gains one-third each. The IRS investigated and issued a Notice of Deficiency claiming Mr. DeMore must report fifty-four million dollars of income, but does not get a deduction or offset for the two-thirds of profits shared by Peters and Wilborn. The IRS admits the venture would be entitled to a business deduction under Section 162, but that deduction amount is disallowed on the basis the IRS has characterized the payments as illegal kickbacks.

It's our position the deficiency amount is zero. No taxes, no interest, no penalties. This scheme was a venture jointly run by the three gentlemen, DeMore, Peters and Wilborn. They joined together and worked together to earn fifty-four million dollars of income over a three-year period, an amount we do not dispute, and split the profits three ways, one-third each. There joining together in a mutual enterprise for profit makes this a classic partnership, in this case, a partnership of crime."

Mr. Simon, beginning with an aggressive, attacking tone, rises and says, "Objection, Your Honor. This is hogwash. There is no partnership. The man stole the money and paid kickbacks!"

The judge, slightly surprised by his aggressive style, says, "Mr. Simon, objections should not be made during opening statement." Pausing slightly and realizing he is with the government and appears in court all the time so he obviously knows the rules, the judge adds, "You of all people should know better. Please sit down."

"But, Your Honor..."

Looking directly at him, and experienced in knocking an aggressive lawyer back on his heals, the judge says with her voice rising, "But nothing, Mr. Simon. No interrupting the taxpayer's opening statement." She looks at me, nods and says, "Mr. Pearson, you may proceed."

"As I was saying, this venture was run like a partnership business, with income earned, special allocations of income and deductions."

"Objection, there are no deductions! He stole the money!"

The judge yells and points her finger directly at him and says, "Mr. Simon, sit down now!"

He drops in his chair and sits down with an audible thump.

I continue and say, "Like any law firm or accounting firm, the venture earned profits and made special allocations to Peters and Wilborn, who took the money first, off the top. Then, the venture had assets that the government seized, which it can do only if the assets are used in furtherance of the criminal enterprise. Since, according to the government's own actions, the assets were seized, they are depreciable and deductible as business assets."

"Where are the assets now, Mr. Pearson?"

"As I said, all assets of the partnership of crime have been seized and confiscated and held pending the outcome of the legal proceedings. Mr. Simon has them, Your Honor."

"Objection to this partnership of crime nonsense! I don't have any assets!"

Fed up with his antics, the judge points her finger sternly and says; "Stop, Mr. Simon or I will have no choice but to hold you in contempt." She looks at me and says, "Continue, Mr. Pearson."

"The government has made clear from the beginning of this dispute, all the regular tax rules apply whether you earn it or steal it. I agree. In this case, the three partners formed a partnership and took a lot of money. Under the partnership tax rules, there are allocations of income and then the partnership computes its net taxable income. With the business deductions it is entitled to claim, the net taxable income is zero. In fact, the evidence will show there is a loss for each of the three years in issue. So, the DeMore's owe no taxes whatsoever and may be entitled to a refund."

"So, if I understand, you're not disputing the numbers but you're saying they belong in a partnership and under the partnership tax rules and regular tax rules, the result at the end of the day is no taxable income?"

"That's correct, Your Honor."

"Nothing?"

"Nothing, Your Honor. No taxable income and no taxes due. Period."

"Well, Mr. Pearson, I can't recall a case where counsel for the taxpayer walks in and says the taxable income is actually zero and I will prove it to you. Typically, it's always some amount of taxable income and the number is a little less than what the IRS is proposing."

The judge removes her reading glasses and looks at me with a kind, curious, approving, expression and says, "I must say you have my attention and I am looking forward to the presentation of your evidence."

"Thank you, Your Honor," I say. I gather my papers and trial notebook and return to my counsel table.

The judge turns from me slightly on her left to Mr. Simon slightly on her right and says in a tone dripping with delicate sarcasm, "Mr. Simon, you may approach the lectern and give what's left of your opening statement."

Mr. Simon walks to the lectern situated between us. His old, scuffed, black shoes plainly visible a short distance from me. His attitude and demeanor match his shoes perfectly. It occurs to me shoes do make the man and this is sometimes not a good thing.

"Your Honor, May it please the court. I have been doing this for over thirty years and I have never heard of such hogwash. I object to everything Mr. Pearson just said. The fact is Mr. DeMore is the ringleader in an embezzlement scheme that netted over fifty-four million dollars from his company, Western Cable. He got the money and then paid illegal kickbacks to the other two co-conspirators, Peters and Wilborn. As the ringleader, he got all the money and paid kickbacks, plain and simple. Kickbacks are nondeductible under Section 162(c)(2) of the Tax Code. This is an open and shut case. Income to the ringleader, DeMore, and no deduction for the kickbacks to the other two, minor bit players. This is all about the central character in this sordid affair, DeMore, stealing the money and being the ringleader in charge. He organized it, led it and gets taxed on it.

I will not waste any more of the court's valuable time because the facts and law are so clear. The IRS wins, hands down. Taxpayer loses. I don't need to remind the Court the taxpayer has the burden of proof and based on the numbers we have in our Notice of Deficiency, we win right off the bat. I have seen nothing from the taxpayer to the contrary, which means I will sit here while taxpayer's counsel flails hopelessly. His battle will be fruitless and the result certain. If it were up to me, we would be done by lunch and we could all go home this afternoon."

"Thank you, Mr. Simon. I must say, I have never seen such two completely different versions and I am curious about how this case will unfold. You have my attention, gentlemen."

Mr. Simon leaves the lectern and I take his place.

The judge establishes eye contact with me, motions with her hand that I should begin and says, "Call your first witness, Mr. Pearson."

"Thank you, Your Honor. As my first witness, I call FBI Agent Jack Ledington to the stand."

Mr. Simon rises and says, "Objection, Your Honor. Agent Ledington is in the middle of an investigation and should not be called to testify."

I reply and say, "Your Honor, I am calling Agent Ledington as a fact witness only. The investigation is over. I need Agent Ledington to testify as to the facts based on his personal knowledge."

In a favorable tone, the judge says, "Understood. Overruled. Mr. Ledington, please take the stand and be sworn to testify."

As if on cue, Jack Ledington rises from a second row bench in the gallery and walks ramrod straight with a slow, purposeful stride to the witness stand. He is six feet, mid thirties, average build, with his only distinguishing feature being a shock of unruly blond hair atop his head. He would not be mistaken for an FBI Special Agent. Maybe that is why he is one. Like police having unmarked cars, Jack Ledington is an unmarked special agent. By the time they reveal themselves, it is too late for the unsuspecting offender.

"Mr. Ledington, please provide your educational background."

"Yes, I have an undergraduate degree in finance and a law degree. I am admitted to practice law and worked for five years as an attorney with a law firm before joining the FBI."

"You are presently in the FBI and specialize in white collar crime, is that correct?"

"Objection, Your Honor. Mr. Pearson is leading the witness and badgering him."

"Your Honor, with all due respect, in our pre-trial conference, Mr. Simon asked me how long I had been practicing law and told me I look like one of his interns. He has not been very nice to me. The suggestion that one of his intern-lookalikes could be badgering an FBI special agent on the witness stand is beyond peradventure."

The judge looks squarely at Mr. Simon leaving no doubt about the meaning of the message and says, "Objection overruled. No more interruptions, Mr. Simon. This is not court-made television."

Mr. Simon sits down with the demeanor of a child who has been repeatedly corrected by the teacher. His act is not working with this judge and he realizes it. He settles in to his chair and puts the back of a pen in his mouth. The pen could have a lawsuit for abuse.

"Yes, I'm a Special Agent with the FBI and I investigate white collar crime, including various types of financial crimes, such as embezzlement, money laundering and securities fraud. I've received extensive formal training on these crimes."

"During the past year, you have been the case agent on the FBI investigation that had Barry DeMore as its primary target, correct?"

"No, not exactly."

"What do you mean by no not exactly."

"Barry DeMore was not the primary target of my investigation."

"He wasn't? Then, who was?"

"Scott Peters was the primary target."

Audible gasp in the courtroom.

"Please explain the background of your investigation."

"Based on numerous tips, we had information and belief that Scott Peters was engaged in money laundering and insider trading. In the course of my investigation of Mr. Peters, I reviewed bank records and stock brokerage records in Peter's name, analyzed telephone and cell phone records for telephones used by Peters, conducted surveillance of him and interviewed witnesses with personal knowledge about the activities of Peters as relevant to the investigation."

"So, your investigation began with and was focused on Peters. What did you find?"

"I found he had large, unexplained deposits of cash into various banks and financial institutions, often under fictitious names or entities designed to hide their true nature. In some cases, these accounts were in multiple off-shore foreign banks to provide confidentiality and insure secrecy."

"Would you describe Peters as being involved in a sophisticated, complex web of financial deception?"

"Yes, that is a fair description. It was sophisticated to be sure. This was not the work of an amateur. There is no doubt he wanted to avoid detection."

"As your investigation unfolded, it was apparent Mr. Peters had devoted a lot of time and effort planning and implementing his activities. He was a man with immense financial acumen. Agree?"

"Yes, I would generally agree. He installed a sophisticated, multi-layered structure of entities and counter-parties to hide a very complex web of deception. He received, invested and transported large sums of money."

"Please describe his life."

"Peters lived large. Larger than life, really. He traveled frequently on a private jet, crisscrossing the country, flying frequently to Miami, Fort Lauderdale and exotic destinations in the Caribbean. Sometimes he traveled with an entourage of fashionably dressed young men and woman. It seems like he used the jet as his personal office and would stay there conducting business while it sat in the hanger. He spent a lot of time at a condo in Miami Beach."

"Based on your observations, the jet was used as a part of the criminal business enterprise. Do you have surveillance?"

"Yes, we documented the use of the jet during our surveillance. It seemed to be flying everywhere."

"Can you describe one activity engaged in by Peters and explain how it worked out to be so profitable?"

"Sure. Wilborn worked at a public company, Amalgamated Cable Supply, as an industry financial analyst. Approximately four years ago, he met Peters and the scheme started small. Wilborn would provide confidential information on the details of soon-to-be issued earnings guidance on Amalgamated Cable and other companies. Before that information was made public, Peters would contact his stockbroker and buy large numbers of put or call options, depending on which way the guidance was scheduled to go. We painstakingly pieced together and matched the telephone records, the bank account wire transfers and the trades in the stock brokerage accounts. They began to line up perfectly and we knew we were on to something.

As our investigation began to unfold, I felt we were on to something really big, that Peters was engaged in significant illegal activity, because the numbers were growing larger by the month. It was like Peters was trying out the quality of the insider information provided by Wilborn and started with relatively small investments. Then, as the illegal information proved accurate, they worked together closely and frequently, like they were in business. After making a little money initially, Peters gathered large sums of money from unknown sources to place huge bets. But unlike betting on chance, he was betting on the certainty of the inside, nonpublic knowledge passed on by Wilborn. I determined Peters generated substantial profits on suspiciously timed trades occurring before the company released its earnings report to the public."

"What was the next phase of your investigation into Peters?"

"I approached Logan Wilborn with the goal of flipping him."

"What do you mean by flipping him."

"That is a term we use in the FBI to describe the point in time in an investigation in which we physically approach a target and turn him or her into a cooperating witness."

"Can you explain how this works?"

"Yes. After we obtain sufficient hard evidence to establish a crime has been committed, we identify one of the lower level conspirators and approach him or her and ask if they are interested in cooperating with us so we can further the investigation. For example, in this case, I identified Wilborn as a lower level player and approached him while he was sitting on a park bench watching his children play. Sitting next to him on the park bench, I explained his scheme had been uncovered and he has been under FBI surveillance for months. To remove any lingering doubt, I showed him a still photo of him exchanging an envelope with Peters. I gave him a choice, which he had to make immediately. Either face prosecution in federal court for federal crimes carrying a minimum sentence of ten years in federal prison, or become a fully cooperating witness with the hope of getting a reduced sentence on a single count of financial fraud."

"So you introduce yourself and ask the perpetrator to become a cooperating witness and assist you in your investigation of others higher up the criminal chain?"

"Exactly. With a co-conspirator's consent and cooperation, we can record his phone calls, wire him for sound and record his in-person meetings and videotape his meetings with others. It allows us to get much closer to the crime and those committing it. We can collect better quality data and increase our chances of convicting the bigger fish higher up the chain of command. We gain real-time access to those we wouldn't ordinarily have access to and evidence of financial crimes as they are being committed."

"How often are you successful at flipping a witness?"

"Almost one hundred percent of the time. The pressure imposed on a white-collar criminal is immense. They are in pursuit of money, while I can convey to them I am in pursuit of their freedom. I explain that, if they don't cooperate, they will be losing their freedom and spending a long time in a remote federal prison where there kids will be infrequently visiting them."

"So Logan Wilborn became a cooperating witness against your target, the bigger fish, Peters, is that correct?"

"Yes, Peters was the target and the main person in charge of this criminal enterprise."

"What happened next?"

"Wilborn flipped immediately after we had our talk on the park bench. He was highly motivated to help us. We met with him for hours as he explained the nature and extent of the scheme, the individuals involved, where the bank accounts and brokerage accounts were located and what they were planning next. Everything opened up in front of us at that point. Then, I recorded calls and conversations Wilborn had with Peters and videotaped pre-arranged meetings they had. It allowed us to get close to the action."

"Wilborn and DeMore were lower down the chain. Is that how you found Barry DeMore, as the result of Wilborn becoming a cooperating witness?"

"Yes, Peters was the big fish we were after and we found Wilborn first and then DeMore last. Barry DeMore was a co-conspirator and one of the three involved in the scheme involving his company, Western Cable. But that scheme was only the tip of the iceberg in our investigation. Peters was involved in this scheme and also many more. DeMore's activities were limited to his company and linked to Wilborn."

"How would you describe Peters?"

"As the hub of the wagon wheel, with many spokes running out in different directions, as he was involved in many different financial crimes."

"How would you describe the activities of DeMore?"

"As limited to his company, Western Cable. He was one of the spokes leading back to Peters, but just one of many. He was only involved in the skimming of profits from the huge cable purchases made from Wilborn's company. He was not involved in the money laundering or other insider trading activities also conducted by Peters. As I think about it, Peters was a conglomerate of crime with multiple entities and ventures and DeMore really a solo act involved in only the one scheme between he, Wilborn and Peters."

"Peters kept the other two in the dark about his other profitable ventures, true?"

"Yes, and when they started to suspect Peters was making a lot of money on other deals, they got jealous and felt slighted. In the end, they felt Peters cheated them out of big money earned in the other deals. They thought they were in, but Peters kept them out and that created bad feelings in the end when everything came crashing down earlier this year."

"How did that make Wilborn and DeMore feel at the end?"

"Outraged, like they had been cheated. They wanted revenge. Turns out, there is no honor among thieves."

"Was Peters on to them as well?"

"Yes, there was enough paranoia to go around, if you know what I mean."

"So in your view, this ended badly with bad feelings between them. It was not like they were lying on the beach holding umbrella drinks and giving each other high fives when they were caught. There was a lot of drama and intrigue, with their relationship in steady decline over the past two years?"

"Yes, that's a fair statement. They were each out for revenge against the others."

"Barry DeMore and Logan Wilborn were the smaller players in the single scheme with Peters, while Peters was out engaging in multiple schemes with multiple players, correct?"

"Yes. I hadn't really focused on it, but when you describe it and summarize it like that, I would agree. DeMore was only involved in and focused on his company, nothing more."

"So, to summarize, DeMore was the smallest player and the one least involved, and Peters was the ringleader, is that fair to say?"

"Yes, that is fair to say. Wilborn was much more involved than DeMore and Peters light years ahead in terms of the depth of his criminality. Peters was definitely the ringleader, no doubt."

"Barry DeMore has been missing since the Monday before the criminal complaint was made public and the other two arrested. Have you or the local authorities located Mr. DeMore?"

"I cannot divulge the nature of police work nor anything subject to an ongoing investigation, but, that said, I can confirm, to my knowledge, he is still missing and has not been found or located."

"After someone is missing for months, what are the odds they will be found alive?"

"In my experience, not very good. Not good at all."

"As each day passes, it becomes even more likely that foul play is involved and he is no longer alive, correct?"

"Yes, as time passes, it becomes more likely, a virtual certainty, a person is dead. If they are alive, they leave tracks and traces of activity we can follow. If they are alive, we are virtually certain to find and locate them. Given time, if we at the FBI want to find you, we will find you."

"In fact, I heard a rumor to the effect that Barry DeMore got in way over his head, got crossways with Peters and took a one way journey on his yacht out to sea. I am sure you have heard similar speculation."

"Again, I can't confirm or deny the substance of an ongoing investigation."

"But you've heard the rumor. I'm not too far off base, am I, Mr. Ledington?"

"I've heard the rumor and no, you are not too far off base. But that is all I can say."

"Changing subjects, do you know why you are here today, what this case is about?"

"Only that it involves taxes due on the money stolen by DeMore. But not much beyond that."

"You may be aware an FBI agent showed up unannounced and told Mrs. DeMore her husband was accused of serious financial fraud crimes, causing her serious, untold, emotional distress which she carries with her to this day. But you may not be aware that the FBI had the IRS in tow and an IRS agent presented Mrs. DeMore a bill for almost twenty million dollars of back taxes due on the alleged ill gotten gains stolen by Barry DeMore. The FBI alleging a crime and the IRS giving her the tax bill for the crime she knew nothing about."

"I was not aware of the details regarding the IRS."

"In your investigation, did you find any indication that Maria DeMore, seated at the table in front of you, was in on, or a part of, the scheme involving her husband?"

"No, there is no indication she was involved. It is just Barry DeMore, not his wife."

"In fact, it's fair to say Barry DeMore led a double life and kept his wife, neighbors and employer totally in the dark, correct?"

"Yes, that is consistent with our investigation."

"And you were the lead investigator, so you would know if Maria was involved, agreed?"

"Yes, I would've known if she was in on it."

"But, she was not in on it, was she?"

"Correct."

"She was the innocent spouse left at home while her husband led a second life of crime."

"Agree."

I walk to the taxpayer's counsel table and pick up Maria's purse.

"Your Honor, may I approach the witness?"

"You may."

I walk toward the witness stand and approach FBI Special Agent Jack Ledington with Maria's purse in hand.

"Mr. Ledington, you watched as I walked over to the taxpayer's counsel table and grabbed Maria DeMore's purse which I am now holding in my hand. I am opening it up for you. Please look inside. Does it look to you like Maria DeMore has twenty million dollars in her purse?" Turning away from the witness and pointing to Maria seated at the table, I say louder, "Does she look like she has twenty million dollars?"

Mr. Simon rises and says, "Objection, calls for speculation."

"Sustained."

I leave the witness and return to the lectern.

"Let me rephrase the question. To your knowledge, Mr. Ledington, Maria DeMore was not a participant in the crimes committed by her husband, was she?"

"No, she was not."

"Mr. Ledington, you served in the Army Special Forces and participated in the invasion of Iraq during the first Gulf War, did you not?"

"Yes sir, I did."

"And you saw the horrors of war where innocent woman and children were collateral damage, did you not?"

"Yes, I did."

"So, you of all people, know the meaning of collateral damage, correct?"

"Yes, Sir."

"Since she was kept in the dark while her husband left to lead a double life of crime, isn't it fair to say Maria DeMore can be viewed as collateral damage to the criminal investigation of her husband? He and Scott Peters were the bad guys, here, right?"

"I hadn't thought of it that way, but one could view Mrs. DeMore as collateral damage."

"If Barry DeMore was the smallest player in this scheme, wouldn't it be a travesty of justice if she was the one left to pay the taxes for a scheme she didn't know about and for income or profits taken by Peters and Wilborn?"

"Objection, calls for speculation."

"Sustained."

"I have no further questions, Your Honor."

I leave the lectern and Mr. Simon takes my place.

"Mr. Simon, do you have any questions for Mr. Ledington?"

"Yes, a few, Your Honor."

"Proceed."

"Barry DeMore was involved in the scheme with the other two to embezzle money from his company, Western Cable?"

"Yes, he was involved."

"This scheme netted a total of fifty-four million dollars over a three-year period?"

"Yes, I believe that is the total number, but I would need to check to confirm."

"Then, he paid kickbacks to the other two, Peters and Wilborn, correct?"

"No, they all got the money, shared the money, but I don't believe I would characterize it as the payment of kickbacks. They were in the deal together, more like partners."

"So, you don't know if the payments were kickbacks or not?"

"No, I don't believe the payments were kickbacks at all. It did not work like that. I know they shared the money equally and they were in the same venture together, with the same objective. Really like partners."

"No further questions, Your Honor."

"You may step down, Mr. Ledington, and you are dismissed as a witness in this trial."

"Let's take an early lunch break. We will resume promptly at one thirty p.m."

"All rise. The court stands in recess until one thirty."

We surround Maria as she gets up from the counsel's table. She places both hands to her face as if she has been viciously struck by the worst news a wife could receive. She has just been informed in a courtroom that her husband is almost certain to be dead, killed in a second life she knew nothing about. She begins to sob uncontrollably, the product of months of pent-up pain and frustration. A volcano of emotions ready to blow and spew. Allison puts her arms around Maria and holds her close, like a loving mother does for a grieving child. The rest of us stand powerless in the face of devastation. I previously told Maria I understood her pain and she told me I couldn't possibly understand. I can see the error of my ways. This is beyond human comprehension, at least mine.

I stand there motionless for what seems like an eternity. Finally, she gains some control and removes her head from Allison's shoulder and says she is so sorry. In unison, we say, no we are sorry for all the things that have happened to her and how undeserving she is of the fate that has befallen her. I wouldn't wish this on her. I wouldn't wish this on anybody. There are moments of sadness in life that defy description or commentary and this would be one of them. Bad things happen to good people for reasons that can't be explained. She then tries heroically to compose herself and Allison hands her a purse-size packet of tissues. She grabs one, then another, and pats her tears as if that will do any good.

She sits back down for a moment and then gets back up to join us, steadying herself against the table as she rises. Seeing my face in front of her, she throws her arms around me and asks me to make this all this go away. I can only stand there, numb. Changing to a more assertive tone, she thanks me for fighting for her and asks if she still has a chance of winning this thing. I tell her "So far so good," and I think we have a chance. Then I catch myself and say, "No, we have more than a chance. We're going to win, Maria." She cracks her first smile of the day. I say, "Let's go get a bite to eat. We must eat to maintain our strength. Winning takes energy."

❖

"All rise. The Court is back in session. Judge Louise Woodruff presiding."

The judge slides gracefully into her chair and after a few moments announces, "Mr. Pearson, you may call your next witness."

I walk to the lectern and open my trial notebook.

"Thank you, Your Honor. I would like to call Allison Broadmore to the stand."

"Ms. Broadmore, please take your seat on the witness stand and be sworn," the judge orders.

"Ms. Broadmore, please explain your educational background and where you are employed."

"I attended the Mary Lawrence School in Connecticut. For the past nine years, I have worked as a private investigator with Watershed Investigations. I have had specialized training in investigation techniques and protocols. I have also had training taught by former FBI agents on the investigation techniques used by the FBI, specifically in the area of financial crimes."

"Ms. Broadmore, your father is the industrialist William Broadmore the third, correct?"

"Yes he is."

"Your father sent you to the world famous Mary Lawrence finishing school, did he not?"

"Yes."

"But you didn't finish because you wanted to strike out on your own and make a difference in the world and help others in a desperate time of need, true?"

"True."

"So, in a manner of speaking, you have unfinished business and have been working tirelessly to help Maria DeMore, an underdog if there ever was one, in her desperate time of need."

"Objection, Your Honor, he is leading the witness."

"Sustained."

"Let me rephrase the question. You are trained in and familiar with FBI investigation techniques, true?"

"Yes, I have had extensive training and experience in FBI white collar criminal investigations as an employee of Watershed Investigations."

"You were assigned and performed the duties of private investigator in the matter involving Barry DeMore. Correct?"

"Yes, I have been investigating the case of Barry DeMore."

"What have you found and have you prepared a written a report?"

Mr. Simon rises and says, "Objection, Your Honor, this report is hearsay and goes to the ultimate facts in this case."

"Motion denied. Any hearsay or other concerns go to the weight of the evidence and I can handle and resolve as the judge during my deliberations. I can fully appreciate the context and its limitations. I will take her report for what it is, the report of the findings of her investigation, and not as evidence of the truth of the matter asserted. Proceed."

"Did you use the same methods of witness interview and document review as that used by the FBI. Is your work as thorough as the FBI?

"Yes, I used the same methods. I spent an extensive amount of time preparing for, meeting and talking with over fifteen witnesses. I prepared a written summation immediately after each witness interview, so my notes and observations are contemporaneous. I was careful to report exactly what they said and I kept my observations separate from the fact-finding element."

"Your Honor, may I approach the witness?"

"You may."

"Ms. Broadmore, I am handing you Exhibit One Hundred Thirty. Do you recognize this document as your investigation report?"

"Yes, this Exhibit One Hundred Thirty is my investigation report for the investigation of Barry DeMore, conducted immediately after the FBI criminal complaint was filed against him and the two other co-conspirators."

I leave the witness and return to the lectern.

"Can you summarize your report for the court?"

"Yes. I personally uncovered the following information based on numerous in-person interviews and reviews of publicly available documents.

Barry DeMore was employed as a purchasing manager with Western Horizon Cable Company. He traveled frequently, leaving his home Monday morning and returning Friday evening. He explained to his wife and neighbors that he was busy with his company's conversion to fiber optic cable. He needed to be at the site of the cable manufacturing companies to supervise and also on location where the cable was being installed. He and the two others, Peters and Wilborn, owned a one-third interest in a limited liability company I call Skimco LLC. Skimco was set up to act as the intermediary. Essentially, it purchased cable at a low price and re-sold to Western Horizon at a much higher price.

Over a three-year period, Skimco netted a total of fifty-four million dollars. Of this amount, two-thirds, or thirty-six million dollars, was taken off the top by Peters and Wilborn. Skimco also owned many assets, including a private jet, a yacht and a condo in Florida, cars and other personal property. Skimco was run like a partnership business, with three partners sharing income and business expenses and business assets. Using the tail number of the private jet, I personally verified Skimco is the registered owner. Using FAA records, I personally verified the flight hours, flight miles and routes flown by the jet. There were other assets owned or used by Skimco and I verified those, as well as reviewing a copy of the condo lease."

“Thank you, Ms. Broadmore. Did you also personally see the documents and schedules produced by the IRS in this matter and marked as exhibits?”

“Yes, I personally reviewed them.”

“Based on your review, do you believe your numbers are consistent with the IRS numbers? You didn’t change anything did you?”

“I believe my numbers are consistent. No, I did not change any IRS numbers. I used them as they appeared. In most cases, it was follow the cash.”

“Where are the assets owned by Skimco now. What happened to them?”

“Immediately after the criminal complaint was filed, the assets were seized and confiscated by the government, mostly by the U.S. Marshals Service, but other federal agencies were involved.”

“Why were they seized?”

“Because they were used in, and in pursuance of, criminal activity.”

“How long will they be held?”

“Until all of the criminal legal proceedings are concluded. Then, they will be auctioned and sold by the asset forfeiture division of the U.S. Marshals Service with the proceeds going to the federal government. It takes sixty days after court order to schedule an auction.”

“So neither Skimco nor the three partners have the assets nor will they get them.”

“Correct. The assets are gone, taken by the federal government.”

“Objection Your Honor. This adds nothing to the record, I could have stipulated to all this and saved the court a lot of time if counsel had just asked.”

“Your Honor, Ms. Broadmore has testified her techniques and methods are as thorough as that of the FBI. Her testimony is as important and reliable as that of Agent Ledington.”

"I agree and for that reason the motion is denied. I will take the information under advisement as the result of Ms. Broadmore's investigation."

"Ms. Broadmore, did your investigation reveal whether Mrs. DeMore knew about Mr. DeMore's criminal activities or benefited from them in any way?"

"My investigation revealed she did not know. Mr. DeMore led a double life of crime and he kept it hidden from his wife, neighbors and even his company. I'm convinced she didn't know and never benefited. Her life was the same, before and after. No change whatsoever."

"This is based on your personal knowledge?"

"Yes, based on my personal knowledge as the lead investigator."

"Your Honor, I move to have Ms. Broadmore's report marked Exhibit One Hundred Thirty admitted into evidence."

"Objection Your Honor. Ms. Broadmore is not an expert and her report contains inadmissible hearsay."

"Overruled. Your objection goes only to the weight, Mr. Simon. I will admit her report for what it is and nothing more."

"I am finished with this witness," as I smile directly at Allison and wink at our inside joke. "I have no further questions, Your Honor."

"Mr. Simon, any questions."

"Yes, just two. You took all the IRS numbers as true and correct and did not change any of the numbers, correct?"

"That's correct. I used the IRS numbers and did not change anything when preparing my report."

"You never met or interviewed Barry DeMore, did you?"

"No, he has been missing for the entire time. I don't know Barry DeMore."

"No further questions, Your Honor."

"Okay, Ms. Broadmore, that concludes your testimony and you may step down. You are dismissed as a witness."

"Thank you, Your Honor."

"The court will now take a fifteen minute recess," advises Judge Woodruff.

"All rise, the court stands adjourned for fifteen minutes."

After the judge departs through the side door, Allison and I lock eyes with a relieved and excited expression. She leaves the witness stand and calmly walks toward me as I stand at counsel's table. I marvel at her grace and professional demeanor. She not only lights up a room, but she can light up a courtroom, I discover. We give each other a big, prolonged, hug, that seems to linger too long if we were just colleagues. I don't care. After what we've been through together in this case, I'm not about to be concerned about appearances. I hope anyone paying attention can see there is something special between us. Courtroom sparks are flying and not the legal variety. I feel it in my soul. I can't and won't hide my feelings. It's too real.

Holding me tightly she whispers in my ear and says, "How'd I do?"

I gently push her away so I can look directly at her and say, "Allison, you were magnificent! Your testimony was strong and consistent and you really connected with the judge. She listened intently to your explanation of the facts. You provided context on what the case was really about. Your conclusion that the scheme was run like a business is critical to our case. That's the key that unlocks the partnership of crime theory. Without you, our case becomes weak and fragile. With you, it's strong and winnable. You're the key to the treasure chest."

She looks at me with large, glowing eyes and says, "Thank you, Jeff. I had moments of doubt, but I looked at your face and just powered on. I borrowed your inner strength. It's like you have some kind of magnetic force field that holds it all together. Sounds strange, but that's what popped into my head."

"With your testimony after Agent Ledington's, the whole case is coming together. The momentum has totally shifted in our favor. We're going to win, Allison," I say gently shaking her with conviction.

"I can feel the winds shift as well. It's like our flat sails are opening up and the winds are filling them. The difference between opening statement and now is palpable. I get goose bumps just thinking about how far we've come."

"Time to win the regatta."

"I'll be cheering you on from the gallery, sailor," she says with a wink as she leaves and walks over and returns to her seat in the gallery with Larry and Miranda.

After focusing on my duties at counsel's table and getting prepared for my next witness, I look around the courtroom and notice there are more people sitting in the gallery. I see some faces that look familiar, and notice Alan Wadsworth, the fourth year associate from the firm, seated in the back row. Our eyes connect and he waves in a manner designed not to draw attention. I am sure he came here for only one reason: to personally witness my courtroom flameout. To the partners at my firm, my DeMore loss will be fast, furious and, for them, free.

I am sure Alan wants to get the news of my demise back to the firm as soon as possible. I imagine him filing a report of my trouncing at the hands of Mr. Simon from the courthouse steps in front of the cameras and bright lights, much like a breathless reporter on the evening news. "This is Alan Wadsworth reporting and it was a scene like no other today in federal court as ..."

Except, I am not following their script. I am following mine. They are in for a really big surprise.

"All rise. The court is back in session. Judge Louise Woodruff presiding."

The judge gets situated and announces, "Mr. Pearson, you may call your next witness."

I walk to the lectern.

"Thank you, Your Honor. I would like to call Miranda Long to the stand."

"Ms. Long, please take your seat on the witness stand and be sworn," the judge orders.

"Ms. Long please explain your educational background and describe your current employment."

"I have an undergraduate degree in accounting and a masters degree in tax from State University. I passed the CPA exam and I am a certified public accountant in good standing. For the past eight years, I worked at Harrison, Cobb & Partners. I am a senior manager in the tax department."

"Do you prepare federal income tax returns and tax returns for partnerships and limited liability companies taxed as partnerships?"

"Yes I do."

"Are you familiar with the partnership tax rules as they apply to business ventures?"

"Yes I am."

"Can you define a partnership for federal income tax purposes?"

"Yes, a partnership is any venture formed by two or more persons with the intent of jointly conducting venture business and sharing the profits among the partners."

"A partnership can easily be formed and has no formal statutory requirements like those imposed on a corporation, correct?"

"That's right. A partnership is the joint undertaking for mutual profit, as opposed to the mere co-ownership of property without any sharing of profit from joint activities. A corporation is a creature of law that can exist only after the filing of a certificate of incorporation."

"Can you describe the requirements for a partnership agreement?"

"The tax regulations provide an agreement to form and operate a partnership can be oral. It does not need to be in writing and it can be amended from time to time."

"So a partnership can be formed by two or more partners with an oral agreement."

"Correct, a partnership can be made with an oral agreement. And the agreement can be later changed by the partners."

"Thank you, Ms. Long. Now, can you explain in general terms, how a partnership computes its taxable income?"

"Yes I can. A partnership first computes its taxable income by adding up all the income it earns for the year and then subtracting its deductions. Then, the resulting net income is allocated to the partners."

"Basically, there are two steps?"

"Yes, a partnership first determines its income and then allocates that income to the partners."

"Is there a form used by partnerships?"

"Yes, a Form 1065 informational return."

"What happens next?"

"The partnership does not pay any tax. Instead, the partners report their share of the income on their individual return. Each partner pays the amount of tax due on his or her individual Form 1040, plus the amount of tax due from their share of the income earned by the partnership."

"And you do this type of work as a part of your regular job as a tax accountant, correct?"

"Yes, this is what I do. I prepare partnership tax returns and individual Form 1040 tax returns for my job at Harrison, Cobb & Partners."

"Lots of them?"

"Lots and lots. More than I care to count."

"Your Honor, may I approach the witness?"

"Yes, you may."

"Ms. Long, I would like to show you a stack of documents and schedules marked Exhibit Twenty through One Hundred. Can you see these documents?"

"Yes, I can see them."

"Are they familiar to you?"

"Yes they are."

I leave the witness and return to the lectern.

"Please explain."

"These documents and schedules were prepared by the IRS in the course of its investigation of Barry DeMore."

"Can you describe what these documents relate to?"

"Yes, these documents relate to a limited liability company formed by Barry DeMore, Scott Peters and Logan Wilborn and used to skim large sums of money from contracts to purchase fiber optic cable and other products and supplies. It was set up to be an intermediary between the companies Peters and Wilborn worked for and Western Cable, where DeMore was a manager in the purchasing department."

"How much money was involved?"

"According to these IRS records, the amount totaled fifty-four million dollars over the three years in issue."

"Did you take the IRS numbers as you found them or did you try to challenge them?"

"I took the numbers as proposed by the IRS and have not changed or challenged them in any way."

"So you accept these numbers and have used them?"

"Yes, without adjustment."

"Can you summarize what these numbers show?"

"Yes, these numbers show Skimco LLC received a total of fifty-four million dollars over the three years in issue. Then, it paid out priority cash distributions in equal shares to each of Peters and Wilborn, roughly six million each year, or a total of eighteen million to each of them over the three years."

"So, the IRS schedules show the tracing of cash paid out to Peters and Wilborn."

"Yes, and I have not disputed them. I followed the cash."

"Your Honor, may I again approach the witness?"

"Yes, you may."

"Ms. Long, I hand you a document marked Exhibit One Hundred Twenty. Are you familiar with this document?"

"Yes I am familiar with it."

I leave the witness and return to the lectern.

"Please tell the court what this document is."

"The report I prepared as an expert in the preparation of partnership tax returns."

"So, this is your expert report you prepared?"

"Yes."

"Objection, Your Honor. This person is not qualified as an expert and her report should not be entered into the record as evidence. It goes to the truth of the matter asserted in this case and should not be admissible."

The judge says in a lecturing, impatient tone while glaring at Mr. Simon, "Objection overruled, Mr. Simon. This is a court of special jurisdiction and there is no jury. Your objections go the weight of the evidence, which I can factor into my decision. There is no good reason why I should be denied help in understanding the case. Further, it is clear to me Ms. Long qualifies as an expert in preparing partnership tax returns because she has done it constantly and consistently for nine years. She sure looks like she knows what she's doing to me.

Mr. Pearson, you may proceed with your direct examination of your expert witness."

"Thank you, Your Honor. Ms. Long, please explain the report you prepared."

"I took all the numbers provided by the IRS and put them into a partnership return format. I started with the fifty-four million of income and divided it equally over the three-year period. Then, following the money and the IRS numbers, I made a gross income allocation totaling thirty-six million dollars to Peters and Wilborn, because they got their money first, in priority. That left the partnership with net income of eighteen million dollars. Then, the partnership had deductions and expenses, including a cost recovery depreciation allowance for the private jet, the rental expense for the condo and other assets."

"Objection, Your Honor. The taxpayer, through the testimony of Ms. Long cannot prove the assets were used in a trade or business. Therefore, the business deductions and depreciation deductions should not be allowed. There is only a gross income number unreduced by any expenses."

"Your Honor," I interject and say, "The assets owned by the partnership of crime were confiscated by the federal government. The U.S. marshals Service seized them and they are in government possession. The government may legally take private property only if the property is used in pursuance of a crime. Since they took the assets under claim of use in the crime, they cannot now argue otherwise at trial. The government can't have it both ways, Your Honor."

"I can see your point, Mr. Pearson. Mr. Simon, where are the assets?"

"They were seized and taken by the government. But I don't see how that is relevant."

"Then, I am going to overrule your objection, Mr. Simon. Mr. Pearson's argument is clear and persuasive. Please continue with your partnership of crime tax analysis, Mr. Pearson."

"Ms. Long, did you obtain the detail on the expense of operating a private jet?"

"Yes. Using the tail number, the FAA has records of the aircraft and where and when it traveled. The hours in the air and flight miles are known and documented. It is a two pilot aircraft, so I determined the average cost per flight mile of operation including fuel, landing fees and maintenance. It is all documented."

"Using the expense and depreciation numbers, what is the ending, net, result for the partnership for each of the years."

"I show no tax due for each of the years. In fact, the numbers actually show a loss realized by the partnership."

"Objection, Your Honor. The taxpayer and the taxpayer's witness have made up these numbers out of whole cloth. There is no truth to them whatsoever!"

"Your Honor," I say in a firm, but respectful voice, "I laid the groundwork and foundation for these numbers used. The testimony clearly shows we took the IRS documents, numbers and schedules as produced to us by Mr. Simon himself, and used them without change or alteration. We followed the cash where it went and we claim business deductions for the assets seized by the federal government. If Mr. Simon has a problem with these numbers, he needs to look himself in the mirror, because the numbers are his, not mine."

"I see your point," says the judge, "and you have made it clear during the presentation of your case that you used the numbers and information as provided by the IRS in its investigation. Accordingly, your objection must be overruled, Mr. Simon."

Mr. Simon stands up and pounds his fist on the table for emphasis and says, "But this is nonsense, Your Honor, with all due respect."

Without hesitation, the judge admonishes Mr. Simon and says, "Your labels and inflammatory words are not helpful, Mr. Simon. Mr. Pearson is arguing based on the facts which I suggest you start with."

Mr. Simon sits down like a chastened junior high school student, the bully who has been forced to back down, and places his pen back in his mouth and chews nervously. From his body language it is apparent his pen chewing is an involuntary response to the pressure he's feeling. I can feel the momentum shift and my confidence building. I'm the winner here and I'm going to seize the day and leave no doubt in the judge's eyes I am confident of my case.

"Again, Ms. Long, to conclude, your calculations show no net income being allocated to the partners from the Skimco LLC partnership for each of the three years in issue."

"That is correct. No income and in fact, the partnership reports a loss."

"And in preparing your report, you used the regular partnership tax rules just like you have done for your clients during the past nine years?"

"Yes, I treated this like a regular partnership, just like any other. No difference."

"Your Honor, I move to have Ms. Long's report found in Exhibit One Hundred Twenty admitted into evidence."

"Objection, Your Honor. This report is biased nonsense. It says nothing and is inherently unreliable. I object to the entire line of questioning and to the substance of Ms. Long's report."

"I'm going to overrule your objection, Mr. Simon. Your objections go to the weight of the evidence and not to the substance. I can evaluate and will do so. Ms. Long's report is admitted into evidence."

"I object, Your Honor," Mr. Simon says while clinching his pen tightly in his right hand.

"Once is enough, Mr. Simon," the judge admonishes.

"I have no further questions, Your Honor," I say.

I gather my papers, leave the lectern and return to my seat.

"Mr. Simon, do you have any questions?"

Mr. Simon walks to the lectern. Wasting no time, he starts in.

"Ms. Long, have you seen the IRS Notice of Deficiency issued against the DeMore's in this matter?"

"Yes I have."

"Does the notice say the DeMore's have fifty-four million dollars of embezzlement income and owe about twenty million dollars in back taxes?"

"Yes, I believe it does."

"So, tell me Ms. Long, which is more reliable. The IRS notice prepared by IRS tax experts after an FBI investigation into Barry DeMore or this scrawny report prepared by little old you?"

"I don't know exactly what you are getting at, Mr. Simon, but I stand by my work. I am very proud of the work I do."

"But the IRS found massive taxes due and you didn't."

"Mr. Simon, all the regular tax rules apply whether you earn it or steal it. In this case, the three partners formed a partnership of crime. Like any law partnership or business partnership, the partnership earned income, had special allocations of income and then had business deductions that offset the income earned. I applied the partnership tax rules and income tax rules like I would for any client. After deductions and depreciation, this partnership of crime had no net income."

"Stop arguing with me, Ms. Long."

"I'm not arguing. I am explaining."

"The IRS Notice of Deficiency has a different result from your report, doesn't it?"

"Yes, it has a different result, sir."

"So, then, how do you explain the difference between a document prepared by a team of seasoned IRS experts and the one prepared by a lowly senior manager in a local accounting firm no one has ever heard of?"

"Easy. I applied all the tax rules that apply when three people get together to form a venture with the expectation of jointly sharing the profits. These three had an oral agreement and divided up the cash based on their oral agreement. They bought assets and used them to conduct partnership business. That is the exact definition of a partnership. It can be nothing else."

"Are you saying you know more than the IRS?"

"I am saying, Sir, I stand by my report. This is a partnership of crime and it reported a net loss for the three years in issue."

"But you just made this up."

"That's not true. I would never do such a thing. I started with the numbers and schedules you provided. I didn't change any of your numbers. Then, I put them into a partnership because that's exactly what happened. These are the facts. Then, the partnership had expenses and deductions from the private jet you confiscated. You can't take it if it wasn't used in the partnership of crime."

"I am going to say it again, Ms. Long. You just made this up."

"I couldn't disagree more. You, Sir, are the one making this up. I'm convinced a partnership was formed and, after proper expenses are claimed, it had no taxable income. If I am wrong, you improperly confiscated the jet and other assets you seized. You can't have it both ways, Mr. Simon."

"You are talking in circles, Ms. Long."

"Let me say it another way. If you took it, I get to deduct it. The partnership of crime had write-offs!"

"I have no further questions, Your Honor."

"Thank you for your testimony, Ms. Long. You may get down and you are released as a witness in this case."

"We will take a thirty-minute recess and then return for closing arguments. The trial is moving swiftly and we should get this case wrapped up much earlier than anticipated."

"All rise. The court stands adjourned for thirty minutes."

Miranda walks toward me at my table with a relieved but concerned look on her face. Her eyebrows are furrowed and wrinkles evident on her forehead. She rushes and grabs my arm with both hands and asks, "Well, how did it go?"

"Awesome, you stood your ground, well done," I say as I stand up and open my arms and give her a big hug. I look her in the eyes and say, "You stayed with your narrative and responded firmly but respectfully. Like a tree against the gale wind, you bent over, but you did not break. You snapped back beautifully. You were absolutely convincing, in my book."

"Thanks, Jeff. He was so rude but you were a calming influence for me. I had my doubts but I had to overcome them in real time. I practiced my testimony and it paid off. I played soccer as a little girl and the coach would always tell me 'practice makes perfect.' I applied that lesson to this project for Maria and it worked!

Now, it's your turn, go get 'em and close the deal, tiger," she says slapping me on the back like we are teammates on the soccer field.

I am shocked and have not previously seen this level of ferocity from accountant Miranda. Maybe I can borrow some of her fire and harness it for myself. Miranda confidently walks away and takes her seat in the first row of the gallery. I look down and focus on my immediate tasks. I gather my papers on the table and check my trial notebook. I need to quickly gather my thoughts for my closing argument. The goal is in sight and I can feel victory at hand.

❖

"All rise. The court is now in session. Judge Louise Woodruff presiding."

The judge enters and takes her seat. After getting situated, she leans towards the microphone and says, "I would like to get this case resolved quickly and am prepared to rule from the bench after closing arguments. I see no reason to wait or delay. Mr. Pearson, you may go first."

I walk to the lectern holding my notes marked "closing argument," which I plan to read.

"Thank you, Your Honor, may it please the court. I will make this brief and to the point, because the facts and law are clear. As the evidence has shown, the DeMore's have no additional income and no taxes are due for any of the three years in issue.

Barry DeMore was not the target of the FBI investigation. He was not the ringleader. He was not the main character in this drama. He was only a bit player, a supporting cast member, who had the smallest role. As FBI Agent Ledington testified, the target was Scott Peters. He was the ringleader in this and many other schemes. As the mastermind, he enlisted Logan Wilborn and Barry DeMore to help create a scheme to skim money from Western Cable. The three met at an industry conference and the plot was hatched. As directed by Peters, the three formed a venture to act as the intermediary. Skimco LLC would buy the fiber optic cable at low prices and re-sell to Western at high prices, netting a total of fifty-four million dollars of income over three years. Following the cash, Peters and Wilborn received their one-third shares off the top. Skimco was then used as their personal piggy bank, allowing them to live large and enjoy the fruits of their web of deception while maintaining anonymity. Skimco bought a private jet that Peters used as his personal office. The others came along for the ride, literally, at times. It leased a condo, bought cars and other assets, all used by them to carry out their scheme.

As FBI Agent Ledington explained, DeMore was a small player. Peters was the star. He kept the other two in the dark on his other criminal activities. As they became suspicious, they became intensely jealous of Peters. Their relationship began to decline and the scheme ended badly. Barry DeMore has been missing since the Monday before the criminal complaint was filed leading many to speculate he may have met an unfortunate demise ending in a watery grave somewhere off the coast of Florida.

The IRS showed up on Maria DeMore's doorstep with a bill for taxes from a venture she didn't know about and income she did not receive. She has been in a double state of shock and despair, with her husband missing as the result of suspected foul play. The daily pain multiplied by the actions of the IRS.

As each of our witnesses testified, the three co-conspirators formed a partnership to carry out their scheme. They acted together with the intention of producing venture income and then sharing in the bounty. Like any partnership venture, this one had income, special allocations of income and deductions. Business income and business expenses. The government seized the assets and there is nothing left.

Whether you steal it or earn it, the regular tax rules apply. Ms. Miranda Long, an experienced partnership tax return preparer, reviewed the books and records and prepared a partnership tax schedule for the partnership of crime. Following the cash, and using the IRS numbers without change, there were special allocations of income to Peters and Wilborn and business deductions for the ventures expenses and assets. The bottom line, the Skimco partnership of crime had no net taxable income for the three years in issue and, in fact, showed a slight loss. When it is all said and done and the dust settles, the DeMore's are actually entitled to a refund.

Your Honor, in conclusion, Maria DeMore is the innocent victim here, collateral damage from an FBI investigation targeting Scott Peters. She did not know about it. She did not benefit from it. She should not be taxed on it.

Using the general tax rules that apply to everyone, we have documented there is no taxable income from the Skimco partnership. Since there is no income, there cannot be any taxes due. Like the scheme itself, the IRS case is a hollow shell that collapses under its own weight. I ask the court to dismiss the case against the DeMore's in its entirety. The tax cloud hanging over Maria DeMore's head must be removed. Please allow her to walk out of this courtroom and grieve at the loss of her husband, without the threat of a tax bill. On multiple levels, this scheme was a loser, taxes included.

That concludes my closing argument. Thank you, Your Honor."

"Thank you, Mr. Pearson."

I leave the lectern holding my closing argument papers in hand. Robert Simon takes my place while glaring at me as if I have just taken his favorite candy bar from his lunch box.

"Mr. Simon, you may now make your closing argument on behalf of the IRS."

"Thank you, Your Honor. I will make my closing argument brief because the taxpayer loses, plain and simple.

Barry DeMore was the ringleader no matter how an FBI agent might otherwise characterize it. He embezzled fifty-four million dollars from his company and paid kickbacks to Peters and Wilborn. He got the income and must pay the taxes due, without offset for the amounts paid to them because kickbacks are illegal. The taxpayer's feeble attempt to call it something else must fail.

The IRS Notice of Deficiency, prepared by IRS tax experts following an FBI investigation, is correct and must be sustained by this court. The taxpayer has the burden of proof to overcome the presumptive correctness of the notice and the taxpayer has failed to introduce any real evidence to the contrary. Barry DeMore stole the money. Barry DeMore gets taxed on the income.

In conclusion, this is an open and shut case and nothing introduced here in court today can change that result. The IRS deficiency notice is correct and the full tax amount is due. Decision must be entered in favor of the IRS, Your Honor. Thank you."

Robert Simon leaves the lectern and returns to his seat.

"Thank you, Mr. Simon. I believe that completes the trial."

The judge clears her throat, moves to the edge of her seat, and leans close to the microphone and says, "As I said previously, I'm prepared to rule from the bench in this case and I would like everyone's attention while I do so." She reaches for her gavel and says, "Order in the court," as she taps lightly.

There is a total hush and the courtroom falls silent.

In a different, balanced, even, judicial, tone, she says, "I have never seen a case where the two parties have such a drastically different view of the facts and law applying to those facts. This is a close case and I can see both sides of the argument. However, at the end of the day, one side needs to win and the other side must lose. Both parties can't be right in their assessment of the facts and law. That is why we have courts in this country, to give both sides of an argument their day in court and a chance to be heard. Then, it is the courts job, in this case, my job, to render a decision.

I will recite my decision from the bench, which will be read into the record as my findings of fact and conclusions of law. My decision will be final.

First, a discussion of the facts. I am greatly swayed by the testimony of FBI Agent Ledington. His explanation that the real target was Mr. Peters and Mr. DeMore was just a small, bit player was an important fact. He confirmed the substance of their relationship, that the three formed a venture to carry out the scheme and jointly worked together to make it successful and share the profits. They each actively participated like partners in a single venture for profit and I cannot find any indication or evidence kickback payments were paid. I conclude as a matter of fact that no kickback payments were made. This information was then confirmed by the report submitted by Ms. Broadmore. She described the venture as if they were running a business and identified the assets owned. I conclude they were in one partnership business venture together and they shared profits as partners.

Ms. Long was helpful when she put it together as a partnership for tax purposes. She correctly defined a partnership as a joint venture carried on for profit. She correctly added there is no requirement the agreement must be in writing and the law is clear there can be an oral partnership agreement that can be amended by the parties. Indeed, that is exactly what happened and the cash distributions were made consistent with their one-third sharing ratios.

As far as the assets are concerned, there is no question the partnership owned assets and there is no question those assets were seized by the government immediately after the criminal complaint was filed. That can leave no conclusion except they were business assets subject to cost recovery depreciation. Similarly, the other expenses of the venture are deductible under Section 162 as ordinary and necessary business expenses. With no kickbacks having been factually made, the disallowance rule of Section 162(c)(2) is inapplicable.

Those are my findings of fact. From those facts, and applying the law to those facts, I find the tax computations prepared by Ms. Long to be persuasive. She correctly applied the partnership tax law to the facts and I so conclude. I adopt her schedules found in Exhibit One Hundred Twenty as my own.

Based on the foregoing, I find the DeMore's have no additional taxable income for any of the three years in issue. Since they have no additional income, they also have no penalties nor interest.

Ms. DeMore, please stand."

Maria DeMore gets out of her chair and stands at attention facing the judge.

"Ms. DeMore at least insofar as your taxes are concerned, your nightmare is over. I find you have no taxes due and I rule in your favor. I order the IRS to withdraw its Notice of Deficiency and end its case against you. If the government owes you a refund based on tax losses, I have no jurisdiction over refunds. You may need to talk that over with Ms. Long, she seems well versed in the tax law.

That concludes the case of Commissioner v. DeMore. I rule completely for the taxpayer. I order the government to take all actions necessary to carry out this ruling.

Congratulations, Ms. DeMore. You won. There is nothing further for you or your counsel to do. Case closed.

The court now stands in recess."

"All rise. The court now stands in recess." The judge rises and quietly vanishes through a hidden side door.

At the instant the Judge disappears, we are like kids released from parental control and finally free to express our inner most emotions. Everyone near Maria remains standing and jumps up in unison with shouts of joy and screams of "Yes, you did it, you won, Maria!" A giant group hug ensues as we are jumping up and down in what can only be described as uncontrolled and unscripted legal courthouse pandemonium. Not one of us cares or is restrained by the normal rules of courtroom decorum.

Maria's eyes are welling up with tears of joy instead of tears of sorrow and the stress wrinkles are less visible. She looks happy and relieved in a way most of us, fortunately, will never have to experience. The weight of the D9 IRS bulldozer has been removed and she has survived the crushing blow and lived to tell about it. She hugs me, and then moves slightly to hug Allison, then Miranda, then Larry, then back to me. She repeats the same words "Thank you, God Bless You," to each of us. She grabs me by my ears and it hurts, like a crazy relative filled with family joy unwilling to let go. Small and slight, but instantly energized, her hands are strong and her grip is tight. She becomes a superhuman superhero of happiness.

The impossible has just become the possible, and the possible turned instantly into a new reality she could not, until now, even think to consider. She will not wake up tomorrow with the dread of the IRS over her head. The clamps of the vise have been removed and she is free to go. Free to walk out of the courtroom a free woman.

This morning, she owed the IRS twenty million dollars and this afternoon she owes nothing, the bill having been torn up and thrown away. It is like the IRS played a giant, twenty million dollar "gotcha" joke and then, suddenly, cancels the game and walks away. "Just kidding," they say as they fold up their tent, pack their bags, pull up stakes, load the station wagon and drive off to terrorize the next spouse of a person living a double life of crime in the next town over. "Have a great life," they shout in unison out the car windows as they wave and drive off and disappear. As unexpectedly as lightening struck her to ruin her life, lightening struck in the exact same place and reversed everything. Statistically, this cannot happen. Here is your life back, sorry for the interruption. Please accept our apologies for any inconvenience we may have caused.

I still have matters to attend to and I pull away from the mayhem. I collect my papers on the table and secure my battle buddy trial notebook. I put my closing argument papers back in behind the closing argument tab, marveling that it must have worked. I look over at the IRS table and Robert Simon and his teammates are dejected and shuffling as they prepare to leave. He looks at me with his soul-less eyes and says nothing. Not even a "good job, kid," bone thrown in my direction. Wearing the same suit and tie, I am sure he will move on and tomorrow will be another day, like the thirty years of days were before. His blank expression fits with his blank personality. He is the most serious person I have ever met, a spot he will not be relinquishing in my mind any time soon. At least I hope for my own sake there are no more like him waiting to appear in my immediate future.

Alan Wadsworth makes his way from the back of the courtroom and gives me an uncomfortable congratulatory handshake, like he is shocked and dismayed at my good fortune. I can see the "how did this kid face the dragon and survive," expression of disbelief. The script he had in his mind was written for my failure. I am supposed to be crashing and burning and getting kicked to the ground. Instead, I am getting hugs and high fives. Graciously, he says, "Way to go, Jeff, I can't believe you won the case. I'm sure Mrs. DeMore is ecstatic to have this cloud removed. I can't believe how much was at stake and I had no idea what this case was about. Well done and I will tell the others at the firm of your great result. See you back at the office," as he turns and hurriedly walks away.

With suddenness, it is suddenly time to go. Maria gives me one more hug and tells me no one would take her case and no one believed in her. Only me, she says. She thought I had dropped her during the long spells when I didn't call. But then I would reappear and then finally instill some small glimmer of hope. She said the case had been a roller coaster of epic proportions, but I was the one constant. She prayed for me. Now, she said, her prayers have literally been answered. And I was the instrument through which God worked. She said she could never thank me enough and never repay me the debt of gratitude she owes me. I thanked her for her kind words.

Then, it is really time to go. When you work on a pro bono case, there are a number of unusual things that occur. One is, there is neither the time nor the money to go out to team lunch or dinner. The celebration ends as abruptly as it begins. Everyone simply leaves and returns to whatever else they are doing. And each person is doing something else at the moment to pay the bills.

With each grabbing an arm, Allison and I walk Maria out of the courtroom and down the hall. Then, turn right and walk out the front of the beautiful, ornate, gold leafed building, and down the marble stairs. We ask where she parked and she points to a weed infested lot about two blocks away in the discount parking section of town. We walk her to her car, none of us able to speak. She puts her old key into the door handle of her old minivan and carefully twists it to unlock the door. Then, she gets in and thanks us one last time. She turns the ignition and a blue puff of smoke emits from the single tail pipe hanging low in the back. Maria clunks it in gear and trundles down the road. We stand waving as if we may never see her again. She is waving her hand out the window as if she knows she never will see us again.

I turn to Allison and I hold her face softly in my hands and say "we did it, Al, we won the case! We really did it!" With tears welling up in her eyes, she looks at me deeply and says, "I want to say I never had a doubt, but that would be a lie. This was a tall mountain shrouded in the clouds we had to climb. No map. No compass. No trail. I am so proud of you, Jeff. You led us up the mountain fearlessly, against all odds." I say, "We did it together and I needed every ounce of your strength of support. There were so many moments when I had my doubts and you were always there for me."

Then we hug and sob and cry. We each cry a lifetime of tears. Frustrations, denials, demands and expectations all rolled into one emotional moment. I never knew these feelings existed, because I was never allowed to feel them as a child. I know Al feels the same way. We stand in that old, weed infested, cracked inner city parking lot for another moment. I can feel the warmth of her soul connecting with mine. She feels glorious and safe and secure. Unlike anything or anyone before.

I walk Allison back to her car. She gets in, starts her car and rolls her window down and says, "I have never been more proud of a person in my life than I was of you today. You took every punch and yet stood tall and delivered the winning blow. You were smooth, yet relentless. I have never seen anything like that in my life. You are made for the courtroom." I say, "Hey, Al, I am not really finished with you. Not yet!" She laughs, rolls her eyes and slowly drives away. She yells, "call me!" at the top of her lungs.

CHAPTER TWENTY SIX

Exhausted after a fitful night of victory sleep, my brain is overwhelmed, the product of sensory overload. I stop at my favorite coffee shop on the way to the office and order my same, boring, Grande Americano. "Yes, I would you like extra room for cream," I say, about the only extra I can contemplate. Yes, I want the room; no I don't want the cream. On autopilot, they ignore my modest plaintive wail and fill the cup to the very top. With the cup overflowing, I spill slightly as I maneuver to my table. I lift the top and see the steam rise. There is a metaphor on display, but I have no idea what it might be. Any extra thought is beyond me at the moment.

I open the morning paper to page two and find the chuckle. I am sure it is funny, but I am not there. I read the prayer and find it food for my soul: "Lord, let me do the work of goodness today." That is definitely the prayer for my yesterday. I read the headlines of the narrow news articles but the words do not connect. I look at the full-page color furniture ads and imagine what it might be like to own a house to put furniture in. The idea seems nearer in my future, although I don't know why. I look down and catch a glimpse my new trial-tested lawyer shoes. They served me well in battle and I am proud. Slight progress measured in inches, but directionally correct. As I get up to leave, I realize my victory coffee does not taste much different from my regular coffee. Life inexorably marches on, whether there is good or bad at the moment. Life is what it is and the rest fits in.

I walk into my office and it is a mess. I have been so wrapped up with trial preparation in my war room; I have had little time to focus on my regular lawyer life. I place my DeMore Trial Notebook on the top of my small credenza, on top of another pile of paper and sit down with a thump and stare straight ahead. I can't focus and I am not going to try. I have unfamiliar lawyer battle fatigue and I need to slowly readjust.

I endure two hours of quiet, mundane associate lawyer paper shuffling and then my interoffice phone rings. I flinch, wondering whether, like a parking meter, my war room conference room time has expired and the receptionist is calling to tell me I need to re-reserve with fresh, new, parental partner approval. I answer "Jeff here," and the receptionist is talking through the plastic phone cover but her words dissemble in my mind. I ask her to please repeat. "Jeff, Mr. Raines is in Conference Room A and he would like to see you." "Sure," I answer with a new type of dread, the kind created by the interest of the managing partner. This can't be good and I sigh.

After a few moments of delay, I force myself to get up and slowly amble down the long hallway to Conference Room A. I have made this trip many times, but now it is dramatically different. Before, I was stressed, but looking forward to winning this thing. Now, I am tense, thinking I must not look forward, but over my shoulder or behind me to see who is lurking. Neither this new thinking nor my new feelings are good.

I walk into the conference room and am shocked by the sight of two large smiles. One of the most genuine ear-to-ear smiles is found on Maria's angelic glowing face and the other smile plastered on the face of managing partner James Raines. I am totally confused by the sight of these two juxtaposed souls representing the polar opposite of my lawyer life at the moment. One is basking in glorious freedom. The other has the look of being forced to be nice by a stern parent. This is a scene I could never imagine and will never forget.

"Jeff, I have a bone to pick with you, young man," he says in a made-for-movie mocking tone.

"Yes, James. What is it," I haltingly respond.

"Please call me Jim."

"Of course, Jim."

"Maria brought in a fresh batch of cinnamon oatmeal chocolate chip cookies that are out of this world. She tells me she has been baking cookies and bringing them to you for the past four months and you haven't given me any. You need to share your client cookies. I am the managing partner!"

"Okay, sure, Jim."

"Seriously, Maria has come here today to tell me about what an incredible job you did on her case. While you know the firm was totally committed and behind you all the way, I had no idea of the complexity and what really was at stake. I knew she had a tax problem you were helping her with, but I didn't realize it was a twenty million dollar IRS problem caused by her husband leading a second life of crime."

"Well, there never was," my words cut short by Jim.

"I know, I was so busy encouraging you and making sure you had everything you needed from the firm, that we didn't have much time left to drill into the details."

"Sure, Jim whatever you say."

"Maria told me the IRS believed her husband embezzled fifty million dollars and was after her for the taxes, because she is married. She said you got up in federal court and said this was not an embezzlement scheme with kickbacks, but instead was a partnership of crime. As a partnership of crime, it had allocations and deductions. She said you found a tax accountant to testify it was a partnership and, after writing off a private jet, there was no income, but actually a tax loss. Did you stand up in federal court and say the scheme was a partnership of crime?"

"Yes I did."

"Did you stand up in court and say not only were there no taxes due, but the evidence will show Maria was entitled to a refund?"

"Yes."

"Jeff, that's the most creative argument I've ever heard of. From a legal perspective, can you explain what happened in court yesterday?"

"We won the case. The judge ruled from the bench it was a partnership of crime and there were no taxes due."

"Nothing, not even a penny of taxes?"

"No, sir."

"What are the next steps necessary in the case?"

"There are no next steps. We won. Case closed," I say flatly.

"Over? No further briefing or post-trial motions? The case is completely over?"

"Yes, Jim, over."

Jim has an incredulous look of disbelief.

"Congratulations to you and Maria. This is an amazing result obtained in such a short period of time. Usually, these cases go on forever.

Anyway, in addition to bringing cookies, Maria would like to share a few words with you."

Maria says haltingly, "When the judge read the verdict yesterday, I was so shocked and overwhelmed. I couldn't speak or even think straight. I wanted to come back to your office one last time to express my gratitude. I need to pause while I compose myself. Excuse me," while she begins to shake and clutch her hands together.

She continues, "When the FBI and IRS showed up at my door I didn't know what to do. My neighbors told me I needed a lawyer and I called the city bar helpline. The first two lawyers hung up on me. You were the only one that would take my case. I had this fear of abandonment driven by what was happening with Barry. I was sure you would drop the case and abandon me. I thought since everything about the case was an uphill climb, you would quit and give up. Then, I thought you would go to court and go through the paces, lose and go home.

I had no idea you would stay and fight, much less stay and figure out a way to win. I could not believe my ears when you presented your opening argument. You told me you were going to win, you told me you would stand up in court and defend me and say there are no taxes because it was a partnership of crime, but had I no idea you would follow through. It is one thing to talk, but another to do it. You have a gift, a drive, a refusal to lose, I have never seen before. I didn't think you would actually defend my rights. But you did and I will be forever grateful. My children will be forever grateful when I tell them this story and then re-tell it when they are older. There is one man out there who defended my rights as a citizen against the government. You.

I wanted one last chance to thank you in person. Thank you for defending little me. I don't know how I got into this mess, but I do know how I got out. You, Jeff Pearson. For whatever reason, you were ready to defend me. It was you who got me out."

Words at such a moment serve no purpose and I had none.

"Thank you. That is all I want to say. I must go now," she says.

"Thank you, Maria. I will walk you out," I say.

Jim says, "Jeff, I have another client meeting and will catch up with you later," as he gets up from the large conference table and grabs the two plates of cookies, like the victor taking the spoils. "Nice to meet you, Maria," Jim says formally as if talking to a corporate executive, "and we wish you the best."

Jim walks out of the room first and we follow, many steps behind. The portly Jim Raines looks goofy walking down a law firm hallway with a plate of cookies in each hand. I will file him in my mental dictionary under "incongruous."

CHAPTER TWENTY SEVEN

The interoffice telephone ring interrupts the dullness of my never-ending document review. Discovery and document production are the bane of every new associate's existence. "Hello, Jeff Pearson," I answer with a monotonous tone. "Jeff, this is Jim Raines, I would like you to meet me for lunch at the City Club today at eleven forty-five sharp. Can you make yourself available?" "Yes, I am available," I say for the first time being invited anywhere by anyone official at this law firm. "Great, see you then."

It has been a month since the DeMore trial and the associates are avoiding me. I see them in the hallway and at the coffee break room, but they do not engage me in any conversations of any import. Since I didn't work on the case with a large team, or any team for that matter, there has been no group celebration. Since the case was pro bono, there wasn't a big celebratory dinner or an all firm all hands on deck party. Nothing.

Before the trial I was the attractive nuisance, the younger sibling they liked to pick on and poke fun of, but that banter has evaporated. Something is dramatically different around here, but I don't know what it is. The barometric pressure is dropping precipitously, but I don't know why.

I feel a sense of discomfort. Like I am the one on the outside looking in. Or possibly it works the other way and I am the one in the zoo on exhibit. I am confined so people can stare at me at their leisure as they walk by. Either way, I feel ill at ease. Maybe my lunch with Jim will change things. Maybe I need to get out more often. Maybe my gut feeling is wrong.

I take the elevator to the thirty-sixth floor of the shiny high rise. This one is made of glass and steel and marble with the lighted pointy top dotting the downtown skyline. I disembark and walk to my left and enter a dark, mahogany wood paneled corporate luncheon retreat. Pausing to take it all in, I walk up to the imposing carved wood and white marble front desk and stand at attention. "Your reservations are under the name of which member?" the receptionist asks. I had no idea these places existed and no idea you had to pay to join so you could pay to eat. I say "Jim Raines," and the receptionist says, "Oh you are with Mr. Raines, his regular corner table is ready and waiting for his arrival. Would you like to be seated or wait in the reception area?" Intimidated by my surroundings, I say, "I'll wait here, until he arrives." "Very well, I'm sure that won't be a moment."

Wondering what will be a moment, I walk over and take a seat on the soft brown leather chair. I sink as I sit and by the time I settle, my feet are barely touching the ground. Lucky I have my new lawyer shoes on or I would look completely out of place. Once situated, I sit and observe while groups after groups of men and women dressed in different shades of blue and gray parade in. Conservative preppy is the order of the day, I conclude. If their individual goal is to blend in with the corporate crowd, they succeeded. Wildly.

Soon, Jim Raines appears bounding out of the elevator and elbowing his way towards me. He must have taken his vitamins and energy drink this morning. He is wearing a brown suit with light brown wing tip shoes. He is the brown outlier in the sea of blue and gray. I will give him credit; he has his own style and is promoting it. To him, brown must be the new black. It goes everywhere and with everything.

"Hey, Jeff, thanks for joining me for lunch on short notice."

"Sure, Jim thanks for inviting me," I say as I stand up and shake hands.

We walk to the table and sit down.

"Have you been here to the City Club recently? It's the place to see and be seen in the downtown corporate business world. Most of the big executives are regulars and it offers great networking opportunities that are important to the law firm."

"No, I haven't been here recently. I've been busy with the DeMore case."

"Well, it's something you need to learn about. Developing business is a key to making partner. Network today and get new business tomorrow. Profits the day after that."

"Thanks, Jim. I will make a mental note and get started."

"Please look at the menu and let's order. Everything is good here, with the fresh fish flown in daily."

I order a house salad with chicken strips and he orders fresh fish with a side of fries. More incongruity.

"Jeff, let me get to the point. I had no idea what the DeMore case was about. I sent Alan over to see how you were doing and he said you did amazingly well. No one at the firm believed you could win that case. In fact, everyone believed just the opposite. It had loser written all over it. Then you pull the rabbit out of the hat as if you are some smiling magician with a magic wand."

"Thanks, Jim. Just doing what I believe I should do as a lawyer. Be a zealous advocate for the client. Nothing too profound, really."

"After the case was over, Maria called and asked to see me. I am really busy but I made time. She was complimentary of the way you handled a very difficult case under impossible circumstances. That is when I asked the receptionist to find you so you could hear it for yourself. Then, we were in the room together and you heard her say you were the only one to believe in her and you had a drive to figure out a way to win when nobody else would even dare consider winning. She repeatedly said you are bold, fearless and gifted. A natural in the courtroom."

"I just did my best, to the best of my ability. No big deal, really. The objective was clear. It was an injustice of the highest order.

I had to right the wrong, otherwise this poor lady and her kids would suffer for the rest of her life."

"I've got some news you'll want to hear. I talked it over with the partnership and we decided to move you ahead of Alan and the other associates and into first priority for becoming a partner. Typically, we wait until a lawyer wins a case or gets a great result for a client. This process generally takes five to eight years and ensures a degree of natural selection. But you broke the curve when you did it in one. So, we want to push you ahead."

"Thank you," I say haltingly. "Do the other associates know about this?"

"Yes, we told them last week. They aren't too happy, but they'll get over it."

"I thought you liked Alan and the fact he was networking with the Capital Industries General Counsel. You said you wanted to give the partnership an update on his activities."

"Sure, but that was before you outran the DFC associate pack with your DeMore victory. I have completely and instantly changed my mind. I like you now, Jeff."

"Isn't this a little sudden?"

"Yes, but it's like a big kennel and the best dog will win out eventually. You're the best dog I got at the moment."

"At the moment?"

"Yes, at the moment. Nothing is cast in stone and things can change. But I'm sure they won't. You're now number one on the partnership track."

"I was wondering why the mood in the office changed. The associates don't talk to me anymore. It seems strained and strange."

"This would explain it. They are well aware and being as competitive as they are, not too happy about it. Some even threatened to leave. But they won't. They'll stay and do whatever it takes to get ahead."

"Is that what this is about? Getting ahead?"

"Yes, it sure is and I'm going to make a lot of money off of your trial skills and I want to get you positioned so I can make the most money off of you as possible. On the other hand, it's a good deal for you because it allows you to get ahead and get yours while you're hot."

"While I'm hot?"

"In a manner of speaking, Jeff. Not literally, of course, but it's a figure of speech. I see this as a 'win-win' scenario. I make a lot of money from you now and you get put on the fast track to partner. Eventually, down the road, you will get yours."

Jim sits back while fine china plates are carefully set in front of us simultaneously by two white-gloved wait staff, while a third observes to make sure nothing spills. "Here's our food. Let's eat," he says, as he slaps me on the back like we're in high school.

We eat and he continues the conversation.

"I plan to get you immediately reassigned to some big cases. If you can win the DeMore case, surely you can win these other cases. I will move other associates, including Alan, off and move you on. Then, when you win the money will flow. It will be disruptive at first, but you all need to learn to get along."

"We need to learn to get along?"

"You know what I mean. We are in this to make money and they will see the logic. I'm putting a winner first, and they'll see the results and get with the program. It might even motivate them to do even more, work harder, who knows."

"What kind of cases will I be working on?"

"I've been thinking about that and I just figured it out this morning on the drive to work. We have a long-time midsize banking client we jokingly refer to as the Last National Bank, or LNB for short. Obviously, an inside joke and we would never publicly say it like that. Anyway, the LNB just got sued by another, smaller, bank and I thought the case was a loser. But not if I have you. With your creativity, I'm sure you can dig through the facts and find some hidden counter-claims and then we will file a huge counterclaim lawsuit on its behalf. The other bank will never see this coming and it will catch them by total surprise. If my strategy works, we can get paid a slice of the counter claim amount we, er you, win. I'm going to assign this loser bank case to you immediately."

"I will be representing our client bank against another bank so our client bank can collect more money?"

"Yes, that about describes it. And, if the money judgment is big enough we can put the smaller bank out of business. Another competitor potentially bites the dust."

"My objective is to extract money from a small bank for the benefit of a bigger bank?"

"Yup, exciting isn't it," he says as he turns away from me and yells, "Waiter, check please!" He turns back and looks at me as he gets up and says, "Now, I've got to run so I can get to my one o'clock conference call. You can stay for desert. Just put it on the tab. They have my number."

I sit alone and stare blankly as he gets up and rushes off saying, "See you back at the office. Put your new banking hat on!" His large brown back disappears quickly as he runs for the exit. It's like watching a brown bear hurriedly running away. I feel like a stunned fish in Professor Abrams contracts class. What happened? What did this mean? I lost my appetite for desert.

As I slowly walk back to the office, my mind swirls with conflicting thoughts. As difficult as they were to deal with in class, my law school professors left no doubt the law was a noble calling pursued by ethical professionals. As a lawyer, you must be ready to defend a citizen's rights, even and especially, poor ones. You must be prepared to use your talents to help those in need and make sure justice prevails.

But in the real world, the task is made doubly difficult because a lawyer must also pay the bills. Paradigms shift and paradoxes appear. Suddenly.

How do I balance between my profession calling for justice and my landlord calling for my rent due next month? How do I zealously represent a bank with money in a fight to get more money? Profits just leapfrogged morality in the blink of an eye. I'm deeply torn and have no answer. Real life is proving to be real messy.

CHAPTER TWENTY EIGHT

I am eager to meet Allison at the bistro for our regular Wednesday evening dinner and arrive early. I have not taken an acting class for would-be drinkers and am uncomfortable sitting at the bar in a tall stool with my feet dangling like a child. Given the choice by the host, I take Option A and ask to be seated at our quiet corner table. Like me, it is small but mighty. I am not bothered by its size but downsize my demands and expectations to fit the space available. I like it here.

Even though I am facing the wall, I can hear her distinct and mellifluous voice rise as she greets the wait staff. They like her and run out to say hello. They should. She is special and lights up a room with her personality and grace. I try not to belabor the point with her, but it is evident she went to finishing school. She is a polished gemstone, set and ready for the rigors of life. She also has an inner toughness that belies her beauty. Don't mess with Al.

She finally makes her way to our table and I rise to greet her and seat her. Her eyes light up and she throws her arms around me. Her perfume has the scent of exotic blended oils, too rich and complex to describe or identify. Her long brown hair is parted in the middle and curls gently down and around her long face, framing her beauty perfectly. I am lucky to be with her. She is the belle of the ball and has likely not spent much time alone. At least not unless by choice. But she chose me this evening and I am anxious to focus, enjoy and revel. She sits down and gracefully crosses her legs as I push the chair in. Her eyes dart over her shoulder and look at me approvingly.

"How are you, Al? How was your day?"

"To be candid, it was rough. My clients and workload at Watershed are evolving and changing in a way I don't like. I'm not having fun at work anymore."

"I'm sorry to hear that. After your nine years there, I imagine you would get the best clients and best assignments. You would have the choice to work on the things that interest and motivate you."

"It was that way up until last year. Then everything changed. I can't explain it, but as I think about it, the changes are real, and for the worse, not better."

"Maybe it's just a phase and it will turn around soon," I say with a hopeful tone.

"Enough about me and my troubles. I hope your day was better than mine."

"My life at DFC is changing before my eyes and in ways I never imagined. It is like the DeMore case represented a paradigm shift where nothing after is the same as it was before. The case fundamentally changed my relationships at the firm and now I can't go back to the way it was before. Bizarre is the only way I can describe it."

"What do you mean? You started out invisible and now you are what?"

"That is a great question and one I don't have an answer for."

"Then, tell me what happened. Do I need to put my English tweed PI hat on to help figure out the mystery?"

"You seriously might need it, yes. And an old English pipe."

"Oh, come on. Give me the facts, Jeffie boy."

"I will start with the latest. This morning, I was toiling away as anonymous Jeff in my office, when managing partner Jim Raines calls and asks me to lunch at the City Club."

"You've never been invited before. What has changed?"

"Exactly."

"Did you go, what happened?"

"I went and he told me I've been promoted to number one associate and the first in line to make partner."

"Are you serious. That's awesome. Congratulations! Let's celebrate!"

"Not so fast."

"What do you mean, not so fast. This is the dream of every lawyer to make partner. What's the catch?"

"There appear to be at least three. The other associates were advised I was moved ahead and they won't talk to me now. The atmosphere in the firm has completely changed and it's because of me and not in a good way. Next, Jim is taking other associates off of cases and reassigning them to me. Some are ready to quit because of the demotion. It's like a competition to see who can become lead dog of the sled and the partners are encouraging it. When I started we were colleagues, now we are competitors."

"Those two are bad enough. What's the third?"

"The third is the most perplexing of all."

"I'm being assigned to work on a loser case for a banking client. Two banks in town are fighting over money, as ridiculous as that sounds, and he wants me to use my creativity to find a winning argument and win the case."

"That's good, isn't it?"

"Not exactly. He made it clear he's using me to make money for the firm. If I win cases, the firm makes big bucks. He wants to use me as much as he can to make as much money as he can."

"You can't be serious."

"I am. Making money just leapfrogged any higher professional duty. Justice and morality have been stuffed in the back seat of the legal sedan."

"I'm stunned. Winning a courtroom drama is supposed to give your career and standing as a lawyer a big boost. These are twists I could never imagine. It sounds trite, but how can something so right go so wrong so quickly?"

"Al, I'm at a complete loss. I want to be promoted and I need to earn money to pay my bills and someday buy a house and all that, but I never thought those necessities would come with this price tag. I need your advice and wisdom. Do you have any extra fortune cookies I can open? What would Confucius say?"

"Confucius might be tempted to say, 'Things messed up bad. Call back later!'"

"I was afraid of that. I can't talk about the firm anymore. What about you, please tell me your life is better and not so complicated."

"I wish I could, but I feel like I'm living your same scrambled version of life at Watershed. Oddly, the conflicts I'm feeling are eerily similar to yours."

"The floor is yours. Please explain."

"I became a PI to help people in need. I want to make a difference. I want to help the underdog, the little person facing the long odds of adversity. My dream was to be a genuine participant, changing the course of history at least for my client and for the better. The Maria DeMore case was the perfect example and you and I did it. We defied gravity and won. That moment we hugged in the middle of the courtroom during the trial was magical. Now, I'm ruined in a sense, ruined by the experience and exhilaration of locking arms with you and marching into battle together. I feel like an empty vessel, serving no purpose."

"I share your feelings. I know exactly what you mean, but until now, I was unable to verbalize. You're so much better at expressing your words than I am."

"At Watershed, I'm stuck working with big, faceless companies trying to chase errant employees or very wealthy soon to be ex-spouses vindictively trying to uncover the dirt on the other. It is mindless, uninspiring work with zero reward. Even if I do a great job, there is nothing to be gained and, in the end, both sides lose."

"Great. So we both are inspired and driven by little guy justice and righting the wrong. But now we're both stuck performing meaningless, insignificant tasks." I break my concentration and say, "This depressing news has made me one thing: hungry. Let's order some dinner. Spinach dip as an appetizer?"

We order and eat dinner.

"Jeff, as I think about it, you started at your law firm with deep concerns about the culture. Your gut feeling was you didn't fit in and didn't belong. Everything, every goal, every objective, was about big billings and big clients. You were convinced you wouldn't last a year in that callous environment."

"True and my worries were real, not imagined."

"Now, everything has turned on a dime. The managing partner himself has named you the top associate over all the others. This is what you wanted. This is the realization of your goal."

"True again."

"The associates and partners made it clear to you: survive or go home. Nothing was hidden or swept under the rug. There was no miscommunication or misunderstanding. Now, you're surviving and prospering against all the odds. Again. It is like you grab adversity by the throat and toss it aside. They set the rules for the game and you broke them. Now, you are the horse they want to ride. Why aren't you ecstatic? What aren't we celebrating at this very moment? I should be raising a sparkling water glass with two limes in your honor!"

"Al, this reminds me of the first time you explained the double life of crime Barry DeMore was leading. I could not wrap my head around it. The thinking, the mindset, was foreign. Where I come from, people only live one life at a time. Now, the law firm situation is foreign to me. I don't get it and it's not the way I think. But you are right, they did set the rules and they made it painfully clear how the law firm game was played."

"Based on conventional wisdom, the firm should be serving you cupcakes with your choice of frosting."

"But the underlying problem is, I was supposed to get in line and fail right out of the blocks. I was supposed to quit and submit, but I can't and won't do that. So, what do I do?"

"I've never met anyone like you before. I've never seen a situation like this. You are like a Coast Guard icebreaker plowing through and making a path where there was none. There are a lot of ships that want to travel through the ice field, but only a few are capable of breaking it up and leading the way. Maybe you're an icebreaker."

"Or a tugboat."

"At this moment, I'm imagining your head sticking out of the smoke stack of the little tug boat. Yes, you've come to life as little Jeffie Tugboat. You are sooo cute," she says with a laugh as she reaches toward my face and pinches my cheek between her fingers.

"Will you put me in the bathtub?"

"If you give me a chance," she says nodding her head mischievously.

"It is getting late and I have new cases to begin tomorrow. I will pay for dinner and imagine a double benefit. Food for the body and Allison Therapy for the soul."

"No fair! Allison Therapy costs seventy-five dollars a session, buster. Pay up!"

CHAPTER TWENTY NINE

I am in my office toiling away. I have deadlines to meet with my existing caseload and I am expecting additional work from the bank case Jim assigned me. My overloaded circuits are set for another helping. This is the work equivalent of eating Thanksgiving Dinner. Every day. Soon, I will need a nap.

The ring of my interoffice phone line interrupts my focus and I pick up the handset.

"Jeff, here," I say using my inside voice.

"Jeff, this is the receptionist and I need to inform you of something," she says.

My mind is racing. Oh, no, it can't be. I'm in violation of some kindergarten rule. Did I run with scissors? Yes, that must be it. Someone saw me run with scissors in the hallway and reported me to the kindergarten police receptionist. I ready myself to confess to the crime and ask for forgiveness. If the punishment must fit the crime, will my scissors be taken away?

She continues and says, "The time on your war room conference room has expired."

I knew it! My conference room parking meter expired. Oh, no!

"Okay," I respond in my most humble lawyer voice.

"You know we have firm policies about reserving conference rooms," she admonishes.

"Yes, I do recall," I say apologetically. "Do I need to ask Lou Stevens or another partner to sign the list and reserve the conference room for me, because I do need it for another case I'm working on."

"No, and that's why I am calling," she says. "Mr. Raines just spoke with me and told me you have permission to reserve any conference room you want, just as if you were a partner. So, while I don't understand, because I know you're only an associate, for whatever reason, Mr. Raines made an exception for you."

"So, I can continue to use my war room conference room without partner permission?"

"Yes, according to Mr. Raines, you may. I will write your name down here for you. Nothing further you need to do."

"Thank you," I say in my most incredulous voice as I drop the phone into the cradle.

I can't believe it, one silly impediment down, only five hundred more to go. I am really making progress and moving up the ladder. To where and for what purpose, I don't know.

I am in my war room. Without cookies and any real legal case hostilities, my existence is mundane and lacks enthusiasm or urgency. I cleaned out the DeMore case files and sent them to the file room for permanent storage. I replaced them with the pleadings and documents produced so far in the case of Bank v. Bank. Jim Raines has instructed me to take this losing case and find a way to win. Specifically, I am to uncover any hidden counterclaims that our midsize client bank may have against its smaller plaintiff aggressor.

I start with one pile of documents and I work diligently to divide them into three smaller piles. I read each pile. I struggle to stay awake.

The small plaintiff bank is a public company, with its stock thinly traded on the pink sheets. I find its last few financial reports and read over the explanations provided by management. I run a computer search of the company and its President, who is also a substantial shareholder. The bank has been in his family for three generations. I find a list of recent Securities and Exchange filings.

I look for problems, shortcomings, or storylines that don't match up. I find the company has had a recent recapitalization done for estate planning purposes and routine warnings of inadequate capital levels required under the banking regulations. There are also indications one member of the Board of Directors is becoming more vocal and taking an activist stance against management on some issues.

I develop some theories and jot them down on my yellow legal pad. I need to bounce them off someone with more experience. I have not had much contact with Lou Stevens since the DeMore trial decision because Lou has been involved in a complex and lengthy corporate securities trial. He just finished a few days ago and is back in the office. I decide to ask for Lou's advice.

I walk to his office and knock with authority on his door and walk in like I'm confident he want's to see me.

"Hi Lou, I need to speak with you about a new case I'm working on. Do you have a moment?"

"Hello, Jeff. Yes, for you, I do and good timing. Just wrapped up that big trial and have nothing to do at the moment. What's on your mind?"

"Jim Raines assigned me to a number of new cases. That's not so much of a problem, except I'm positioned ahead of and sometimes instead of the other associates. I guess I should be happy because it is progress for me, but I don't feel good about what has happened to the other associates. They won't talk to me."

"How do you feel about it, Jeff?"

"Not very good. I feel we should be colleagues and not competitors. On the same team, instead of pitted against each other as if we are on little separate teams."

"I thought that would be your answer. From day one, you've been different. You care about the law and what is right. You want to see justice done. You are not out to make the most money, but you are out to do the very best you can for your clients. Our oath as lawyers requires us to zealously represent our clients within the bounds of the law and I think of you when I think of those words. You're a zealous advocate, but with a strong sense of fair play. Honor and dignity mean something to you."

"Thanks for those kind words. I had no idea what you thought of me, other than as a newbie lawyer pestering you for help. I thought I was a rock in your shoe. An annoyance."

"I treat you that way because I care deeply about you. If I didn't care, I wouldn't say a word. It's the opposite of what you think. I like you and want you to succeed at the highest level, like you did it in the DeMore case. That's your destiny."

"I must say I'm surprised. Kind of a strange way to show someone else you care, but I guess you are like the coach who is yelling at the player to get the most out of him."

"Exactly and I see a little of me in you. I started out bright eyed and bushy tailed and ready to take on the world, just like you."

"You see yourself in me, really?"

"Yes, I do. The similarities between us are striking and have caused me to reflect about my career. I've done some real soul searching in the past few months."

"I'm sure we can save that discussion for another day. I have some questions about this new bank case and I would like to ask your opinion about what to do."

"Sure, happy to help. As I said, I have nothing better to do at the moment," he says as leans back in his large leather office chair and puts his worn shoes on the top corner of his desk. He looks up and stares at the ceiling. I curiously glance up and see nothing there.

"A small, family-owned bank has sued our midsize bank client for a relatively small amount of money. It looks like their claim is a winner. Jim Raines asked me to take a look and see if I can use my creativity to find a counterclaim that our client could file against the smaller bank. If so, he thinks we can get additional fees if the counterclaim is successful."

"I've heard Jim take this approach before. This is not unfamiliar to me. Continue."

"I read through the file documents and searched the public records. It looks like there could be at least one basis for potential counterclaim liability. The small bank just completed a recapitalization done for estate planning purposes and has warnings of potential inadequate capital. There is also one member of the Board of Directors that may not always vote with the others. If we could establish the recapitalization was not done for the benefit of the company and is somehow connected to the claims of inadequate capital, there could be some potential liability here. In addition, the company is a small family owned company and the stock is thinly traded. This could add a second element to the mix."

"How do you feel about this line of counter attack?"

"To be candid, not very good. I think we're trying too hard in the case and distracting from the main issue. The small bank sued our client for what appears to be a legitimate claim and the facts and law align with their pleadings. I think we're grasping at straws. We can adequately defend our client on the main case and let the chips fall where they may. I don't see any need or justification to try and launch a counter attack by using a counterclaim approach."

"What's your advice to the client, as you think it through?"

"After I explain the options to the client so they are fully apprised, my advice is to defend on the merits and try to settle as quickly as possible. This will keep the costs and fees down and allow our client to get this resolved quickly so it can move on with its business. I don't see any reason or justification to make this bigger than it is. Our client has a narrow interest as a defendant and we should keep it narrow."

"Well done. Spot on."

"What do you mean?"

"That's precisely the way I would've analyzed the case when I was your age."

"Thanks Lou. Your positive words mean a lot. I value your opinion."

"You value my opinion, do you," he says, as he takes his feet down from his desk, straightens his chair behind his desk and fixes his eyes directly on mine. His smile evaporates and in his most serious tone, he says, "Then, let me share something else with you."

"Please do," I say fearful of what's to come.

"I have a recommendation for you," he says as he puts both forearms on his desk and leans forward on the edge of his chair to get closer to me.

"What is it?"

"Leave," he says abruptly.

"What did you say?"

"I said leave and do it soon," he says using his deep trial voice.

"I'm shocked. What are you talking about? I thought you like my work. I thought you respect me for how I handled and won the DeMore case. How could you say this to me?"

"I'm saying it to you because I care more for you and about you than you could ever imagine."

"You do? Now I'm really confused," I say as I throw my hands in the air.

"Let me explain," he says as he moves so he is sitting sideways to his desk, facing in my general direction, and begins to rock back and forth. "From all outward appearances, I am a successful lawyer and have made a lot of money here at Dewey Frederick. I give speeches, write scholarly articles and am named to every outstanding lawyer list there is. But it has all come at a price, an enormous price. This place has extracted a heavy toll on me and basically sucked the life out of me. Everything here is about the billable hour, the big clients and the big fees. Once you get on this treadmill it is virtually impossible to get off. I don't want you to make the same mistake I made."

"What do you mean? Don't you think I am capable of doing the job and making the grade here?"

"You're enormously talented and have a tremendous future. That's why I'm telling you to leave while you have the chance.

Otherwise, like me, you'll be stuck here forever working at the direction of Jim Raines trying to figure out how to get more money out of the practice of law."

"This is not the message I expected to hear. I was beginning to feel like I could do it."

"That's why I'm talking to you, kid. There are things you don't understand about life and this firm."

"Like what?"

Holding out his left hand and pointing to his left side behind his desk, he says, "Do you see my college bulldog sitting on my credenza?"

"Yes, and I wondered why on earth you have a bronze bulldog there."

"That little bulldog is the only object in this office that brings happiness because he reminds me of my law school days and the early years of practicing law. He reminds me of when I was you. And I will never get those years back. I have never admitted this to anyone, but I have serious regrets about my life. I learned this all too late, but you don't have to. You don't have to commit the same mistakes I did. Please take my advice. For the sake of your future, move on and up and out."

"It's not in my nature to quit."

"Every rule has an exception. Make this one yours," he says, as he folds his arms across his chest.

"But you have done so well here. It's not as bad as you say it is, is it?"

Realizing I'm a little thicker headed than even he imagined, he shifts gears and says, "Jeff, do you know what's in my credenza, immediately below my bronze bulldog?"

"I imagine you have file drawers in your back credenza filled with important papers."

"Good guess and that would be logical," he says, as he pushes back from his desk and turns to the left side. "Stand up and step around my desk and stand near the credenza while I open the side drawer."

"Okay, if you insist," I say, as I stand up and walk around while he opens the drawer.

"What do you see," he asks as the drawer opens with the loud clank of glassware.

"I see a lot of bottles of hard liquor."

"Look closer."

"I see large bottles half empty or less. The drawer reeks of the smell of a liquor cabinet."

"Let me show you the other drawer," he says, as he closes one and opens the other.

"What do you see?"

"Small glasses for hard liquor drinks. Soda and mixers and a full bar."

"What you don't know is I have a serious drinking problem," he says, as he closes the drawer and motions me to return to my seat in front of his desk. "I always thought I could handle the booze, but lately it has handled me. I drink more and more frequently to medicate my problems and take away the pressure and pain of life."

"I'm surprised but I guess I shouldn't be. I took an ethics course put on by the State Bar and they devoted half the time to substance abuse. They mentioned this was a serious challenge for many lawyers. I had no idea."

"They were talking about me, Jeff. They were talking about lawyers like me. There are many others like me, too, unfortunately."

"I had no idea."

"I hide it well."

"Is there anything I can do to help?"

"No, this is my problem and I need to deal with it and get the help I need. But I was you once, and I don't want you to end up like me. Don't do it. Please learn from my lessons, don't repeat them. You have unbelievable talent and don't waste it here. Fulfill your destiny and to do so, you must go elsewhere."

"Thanks, Lou. I don't know what else to say."

"Don't say anything. Find your next opportunity and leave to pursue it. A great life requires you face and make difficult decisions. Someday, you will thank me for this talk and the advice. You asked for my opinion and there, I've given you the best I have to offer. Nothing held back. Full stop."

"Do you have any other advice for me?"

Pause, while Lou gazes at nothing on the ceiling and contemplates the question deeply with a wrinkled look on his forehead.

"Yes, as a matter of fact, I do. Judge a book by its cover."

"What?"

"I said judge a book by its cover. I'm speaking about books. Now, get out of my office," he says, as he waves me away with his hand.

I stand up and slowly inch backwards towards the door in a state of total, utter, disbelief.

"You, of all people, know I don't like to be sentimental or use more words than necessary. Make yourself scarce," he says, as his eyes narrow and he turns away and lowers his head to focus on the papers on his desk. He looks like a wise old rumpled elf.

"Will do," I say, as I turn and walk out for what I realize may be the last time and close his office door behind me.

I take a few steps and then stop in the hallway and turn and lean against the wall. The intensity and weight of the message sinks in as I place my right hand to my forehead. My goal when I started this long journey was to get into law school and now I am told to get out? I can't be both in and out. Both can't be true. The incongruity is magnified by the moment. Cognitive dissonance at its finest. My head is pounding. I have a migraine. A great life requires you face and make difficult decisions, he tells me. Easy for him to say.

CHAPTER THIRTY

I gently push the small rowboat off from shore on the tranquil, magical, waters of Seeley Lake in Western Montana. Al is in command of the ship. She is seated in the middle with the oars in hand. We are at her most favorite place in the world. I hop in and carefully move around her and take my passenger seat in the front as the boat glides silently away from the shore. I look straight ahead, mesmerized by the sight of crystal clear water running up to the tall mountains. Like a curious child, I stare down into the water and see the lake bottom in vivid detail at a depth of five feet, then ten feet. I touch the surface with my fingers and feel the frigid mountain water. I see schools of fish of every size. Viewing from the starboard side of the boat, I see the brilliant colors of rainbow trout swimming aimlessly. They are no doubt ecstatic and happy with their perfect high rocky mountain world. I can make believe and assume, anyway. I take a deep breath and smell the freshness of the surrounding pine forest.

This clear blue-sky day and not-to-be-believed scenery should be made into a television commercial or possibly a post card. I would send this picture postcard to my close friends at home with the words "wish you were here," and mean it.

I interrupt nature's silence and say, "I like it when you row."

"You should."

"Your rowing strokes are fluid and consistent. Barely a ripple."

"I have lots of experience. I'm pretty good, if I do say so."

"Who taught you?"

"A rowing instructor with crew experience at summer camp."

"I should have known. You have been professionally taught everything in your life, it seems. Did you have lessons for everything as a child?"

"Yes. The best."

"Dance, violin, piano, soccer, chess?"

"Everything except chess. That was for nerds."

"It took this boat ride for me to learn something new about you. I will add this tidbit to my expanding knowledge base. Debutantes-in-training don't do chess."

"That would be true. Takes too much time and the little pieces get lost."

"Stop rowing for a moment, and turn around and face me," I say in a calm and caring tone.

"Okay, I will move to the back of the boat so we don't tip over. I don't like to get dunked in the frigid water. Tried it once as a little girl and have no desire to repeat."

She moves from the middle seat to the back seat and faces forward. The boat rocks gently. We are looking at each other from opposite ends.

"I want to ask you a serious question."

"Uh, oh. This can't be good. From my experience, when you want to get serious, it is no laughing matter."

"Ha. I want you to think back over your life. You had everything a person could possibly want and your father laid out your life plan. All you had to do was fall in line and follow along. Why didn't you do it? Why wasn't his plan good enough for you?"

"Great question and one I've given new thought to. When I was about three-years-old, I liked to go outside and dig. It was spontaneous and unstructured. There were no rules. No beginning, no end. Simple exploration. Life was in front of me. I determined the direction to be taken next. I wanted trucks and shovels so I could make roads and bridges. Later, I dug a small pond and put water in it. I had little houses placed neatly in a row and the makings of an entire neighborhood. My mother and housekeeper would interrupt and yell to get me to come inside, but I refused. I was having too much fun. They would scold me for getting dirty and would repeatedly tell me to 'Get inside and wash your hands young lady.'"

"I'm confused. What does digging as a three-year-old have to do with your life and the struggles with your father?"

"It has taken me most of the rest of my life to figure that out. But I have pieced it together and now my life makes perfect sense. Finally, I get it."

"Maybe for you, but you lost me. Can you explain to Jeffie boy here? I tend to think in two dimensional black and white."

"When I was three and at play I was being authentic. That happy little girl is who I am. It was the expression of my true self. The life my parents created for me was based on my parents dream, not mine. If they had paid attention, they would have encouraged that little girl to be a digger, in a manner of speaking. The time I spent alone was therapy for my soul and the authentic expression of what made me happy. The world they created was fiction to me, one they created based on what they wanted. It was all about them and nothing about me."

"Continue."

"This set the stage for a conflict of historic proportions. They thought that by providing everything for me, I would be happy. And the more I had, the happier I would be. Or so the logic goes. But they were just providing more of what I didn't want. It was like they were baking raisin cookies for me and I hated raisins. In the face of wealth and power, how does a child speak up? How does a child even know how to speak up under any circumstances, let alone mine?"

"Wow. This is profound and I've not thought about my life at this level. This is a depth I have not plumbed. Please explain more."

"I had everything but nothing at all. The more tangible stuff I received the more internal conflict it created within me. I didn't know or understand at the time, but I have since put the pieces of the puzzle together."

"And if I had to pick a puzzle picture for you, Al, it would be Seeley Lake. You are a natural beauty."

"Thank you. That is the nicest thing anyone has ever said to me. And since we are here, I know you mean it. I always feel deeply connected to this place in a way I could never explain. Unlike all the stuff of my confused childhood, this place anchors my soul. I'm at peace here. I feel serene in the midst of nature. So, yes, I agree, this would be a perfect puzzle picture for me."

"At what point in your life did you begin to understand the source of your conflicted feelings and then act upon them?"

"In college, when I was sent away to finishing school. It was a well-intentioned environment, but not for me. When I was living away from my parents in Connecticut the light bulb went off in my head. I enjoyed my freedom and I liked being alone. With all the activities in my childhood, with every minute planned in advance, I was overwhelmed and exhausted. I was eighteen and worn out. Like a high mileage sports car, I imagine. I had long conversations with many other girls and I discovered they felt the same way I did."

"What happened next?"

"That's when I started looking for a summer job and found the private investigation firm. It provided me with everything my life didn't. Freedom, adventure, unpredictability, you name it. Once I started I was hooked. I found my true calling. Helping the person in need at a time of crisis. It was the perfect storm of problems circulating in their life that caused them to need the help of an investigation firm. Something was really wrong, really broken and they needed someone to help them fix it. My life was perfect and, at least on the surface, never needed fixing. I desperately wanted to help others and, in the process, help myself, but I never had the chance. I was like the glue in search of the broken vase."

"Interesting analogy. Continue with your thoughts."

"Being at an investigation firm was the ideal job for me at that point in my life, my time of need, I guess you could say. So, it was a two-for-one deal. I got to help others in their time of need, while I was being helped in my time of need. Worked perfectly."

"How do you feel now about your life and your career?"

"I will answer that in a minute. But, before I do, I want to ask about your childhood, going to law school and working as a young lawyer. As you describe it, you had the opposite childhood I did. What was it like and what have you learned?"

"This is one of the reasons you make a great investigator. Excellent interrogator. If you were questioning me under the bright lights, I'm sure I would confess, without even knowing it."

"True. I'm good at getting to the bottom of things and will stop at nothing until I do."

"From age nine, I didn't speak to my mother because she seemed to be incapable of saying much of anything and I didn't want to speak to my father because he was capable of saying too much, in angry bouts of rage. Neither extreme was good. It was a world you wanted to run from. The first objective was to survive, then the second objective was to escape."

"I'm sorry. Your problems make mine look small."

"Thanks, but the challenges were real to us both. No need for relative comparison here. Anyway, my upbringing created a drive to survive. I cannot stand it when I see the little guy being overwhelmed and controlled by the one in a position of power. That, in turn, creates a burning desire to figure out the one way to win and there is always a way, no matter how remote the possibility. Impossible odds mean nothing to me because that's what I've faced my whole life. It may start with adversity, but I won't let it finish that way. With persistence, I can and will affect the outcome of the game. Through shear will I will bend the arc in some fashion."

"So, you had to fight hard to get everything you have. Nothing was given to you."

"True."

"But then on the way up the ladder, you accomplished your goals faster than you ever imagined, and that created a new set of problems for you, didn't it?"

"Yes. The ultimate paradox appeared. Imagine this scenario. I wanted to take the DeMore case and I wanted to win. The law firm didn't want me to take the DeMore case and did not want me to win. The whole case was built for intractable conflict. It was like there were two tectonic plates colliding and pushing in the opposite direction. Eventually, one side had to give way to the other. What's interesting about this scenario is they set the rules and the game was rigged in their favor. However, while they weren't looking, I hopped over the fence, ran out to battle and prevailed against impossible odds. The ending was not according to their script."

"What did you learn?"

"I learned adversity is a fact of my life. But I will not give in to adversity. I want to face it and then figure out how to turn it to my advantage. In nature the most amazing plants and animals survive under the harshest of conditions and I want to be one of those survivors. But then, having reached that level, mere survival is not enough. I want to prosper. In order to prosper, as Lou advised me, I had to leave."

"That was hard for you wasn't it?"

"Yes, one of the hardest things I've ever done. I thought I could survive anything and maybe I can. But the price of that kind of survival is too high. That is one of the messages Lou delivered to me. He wants me to reach my full potential as a lawyer, but he didn't want me to pay the same price he did. He didn't want me to make the same mistakes and end up the same way as him. He cared enough, loved me in his own gruff way, to tell me the secret he has harbored and never told anyone else. He wanted me to learn my lessons early, not late. He wanted to save me from his fate."

"You quit and left the DFC law firm."

"Yes, as amazing as that sounds, I did. Lou told me to make an exception to my 'I will never quit' rule and he was right. He is my Confucius come to life. I had to turn his words into action. They were too valuable, too real, to ignore. My risk was in doing nothing, inaction, rather than action. Another paradox, I suppose."

"It seems the case that paid nothing provided you with everything. The bank case that paid you everything provided nothing. Imagine, you could still be there trying to get more money for a bank with money all for the benefit of Jim Raines. The irony seems beyond description."

"Yes, my last assignment was to find a creative way for one bank to get another bank's money. I can only chuckle at how nonsensical that sounds."

"Are you glad you left?"

"More relieved than anything. I had to leave. I couldn't stay. I would have had a target on my back with the other associates, as sad as that is to say of folks I thought of only as my colleagues, and been miserable working on meaningless cases for meaningless clients. That's why Lou showed me his liquor drawer with the headline 'Don't Be Like Me,' and the byline 'You Can Do Better Elsewhere.'"

"What was the bigger message Lou was trying to convey?"

"Great question. Probably, that a great life requires you face and make difficult decisions. But to do so, you need something that's in short supply. Courage. Turns out, it takes a lot of courage to act on your convictions."

I stare at the mountains in a moment of deep reflective thought.

"I have a question for you, Al," I say. "How is it possible we each started life's adventure as children from opposite ends of the spectrum, yet end up in the same boat, so to speak?"

"You have an allegorical way about you, Jeff."

"Thanks. I like being in your boat, by the way."

She looks up and castes a blank stare at the mountains in the distance.

"As I think about it sitting here in the midst of nature's silence floating aimlessly, it seems we each had to 'right the wrong' we experienced growing up by 'righting the real wrong' experienced by Maria. Her case of unbelievable personal pain and anguish was the tool we used to fix our own lifetimes of pain. Three painful existences, three tortured souls, inexplicably became intertwined for a period of months. Then the pain went 'poof' with the reading of the decision by Judge Woodruff. Intractable problems faced and resolved in mystical fashion."

"How do you feel about the decision and chaos that followed?"

"I feel liberated by the decision. To reach my potential, I need to leave my firm, Watershed, in my rearview mirror. Time to move on and up. Time to reach the potential of my life. With how and what, I don't know. I'm excited for the next adventure, whatever that may be."

"Well spoken. You can be the captain of my ship anytime."

"What are we going to do now," she says turning her head in a playful manner.

"What do you mean *we*? Do you have a mouse in your pocket?"

"You better not turn into Lou Light, Mr. Wiseacre, or I will club you with this oar!"

"Well, if you make me be serious, we have this fabulous relationship born of adversity that we should tend to. I say we turn adversity to our advantage and focus inward. Just us. Interested?"

"Maybe. Tell me more," she says with a broad smile, twinkling eyes and with one hand slowly twirling the end of her long brown hair.

"At this moment, Confucius say: 'Where ever you go, go with all your heart.' I'm going to obey the words of Confucius and follow my heart. But to do so, I need your help. I can't do it alone. What do you say?"

"He's too wise! I can't argue with the words of Confucius," she says, as her face lights up like a candle and her smile extends from ear-to-ear.

I reflect as the magnitude of her gift soaks in and my spirits soar. This is now my favorite place in the world.

"If I do what I want to do at this moment, I will rush you and the boat will capsize. You told me you only want to get wet once. So, exercising restraint, would you like me to start rowing?"

"That would be nice, but I'm not moving from the back of the boat."

I get positioned to row in the middle seat and face the back of the boat.

"You are one lucky girl," I say with lawyer confidence. "You can see the lake, the mountains and me. You get to look at all three."

"You are one luckier boy. You only get to look at me!"

I discover I'm looking at my puzzle picture. Allison's natural beauty framed and surrounded by the natural beauty of this setting. Both will live in my heart forever and neither would have been possible had I continued to pursue my original notions of success. Lou was right. A great life requires courage.

About The Author

A simple storyteller armed with warmth and humor, Fred has written three nonfiction books. This is his debut novel. He is a lawyer and has been recognized as an outstanding alumnus of Lincoln Southeast High School and the University of Nebraska Lincoln. He has written numerous articles on federal tax matters and given over three hundred speeches on topics such as tax reform before professional organizations. For more information, visit www.fredwitt.com.

42981273R00149

Made in the USA
San Bernardino, CA
11 July 2019